Fakers, Breakers, and Takers

SERINA GARLAND

This is a work of fiction. Names, characters, businesses, places, events, locales, and incidents are either the products of the author's imagination or used in a fictitious manner. Any resemblance to actual persons, living or dead, or actual events is purely coincidental.

For permission requests, write to the author, addressed:

"Attention: Permissions Coordinator", at the address below.

Infinity Publications, LLC.

Vanderbilt Media House, LLC.

999 Waterside Drive

Suite 110

Norfolk, VA 23510

(804)286-6567

www.vanderbiltmediahouse.net

Library of Congress Control Number: 2022907254

ISBN-13 : 978-1-953096-25-8

First Edition : July 2022

10 9 8 7 6 5 4 3 2 1

This book was printed in the United States

Scriptures marked KJV are taken from the KING JAMES VERSION

Dedication

This book is dedicated to my Lord and Savior Jesus Christ, for without His Love, Grace, and Mercy my words would not have received life.

Ladies and Gentlemen if you read my book, you are in for a ride. Please stop and seek help with guidance before giving away your soul to a *Faker, Breaker, or Taker* only to be trapped with an *Aker*.

Acknowledgement

First and foremost, I want to give Honor to my Heavenly Father who believed in me, when I didn't believe in myself. I would often hear His voice in my head, reminding me to finish what I started.

To my daughters, Shantaya M., Stephanie M.A., and Kiana S. Tabb. I appreciate you for the many times I nagged you to read, edit, and listen to my story. *"Mommy truly Loves you all!"*

To my husband, Mark L. Garland, for all of his unconditional love, inspiring words, and his motivational support along with our prayers together.

To my sister, Casandra Harris, for pushing me to get this book out and especially her editing skills toppled with her honest advice on how my book sound.

Last but not least...To all those who believe in me. Thank you!

Food For Thought

In coming up in today's world, many of us grow up in shattered homes, where physical and mental abuse plays a part in our emotional growth and outcomes. Many of us are lacking the love and attention we crave from our parents, who we depend on to protect us from dangers seen and unseen?

We rely on them to provide, teach, and guide us down life's roads. Hoping and praying that they would fulfill the tasks God so entrusted upon them to do. So, when taking on a big responsibility, it is truly a gift from God. We may think that we choose our paths, but God plans our destiny, steps, and outcomes.

In staying on the right path, God will give us the gift of righteousness, so we can become righteous in what we think, say, and do. Many mothers as well as fathers should raise their children with morals and values teaching them the right choices in life so that they grow up respecting, appreciating, and loving them for who they are and what they have instilled in them.

Many women talk of the wonderful gifts God has bestowed upon them however when giving such gifts that some undeservingly deserve, they fail to protect and shelter it as the most important task at hand.

Prime example of God's unmerited *favor* is when God gives us all a gift that we truly didn't earn, he still gave in spite of our sins.

Introduction

If we took more time in understanding and seeking after God, we will be prepared for the challenges and trials we are about to face. If many of us were enlightened on the games of an aker beforehand then many of us wouldn't be in some of the situations that we are in today, trying to find out how to get away from the fear that has us trapped within.

We need to stand strong on what we believe in and stop being deceived by *Fakers, Breakers, and Takers* who will take advantage of your lack of power that you should obtain. Most of us have seen many things in our lives that have scarred, frightened, and left us screaming for help.

Baffled by the things that we have seen and the *stuff* that we have heard, our minds are filled with negative thoughts on what to believe. As to where Moms are supposed to tell her little girls about the birds and bees and never to let a man take her for granted. Reminding her that the Bible says that when a man finds a woman, he finds him a good thing.

As to where the fathers should teach their sons how to be firmly established. Teaching them how to be men by the example they put in front of them. If you don't get your lives under control then your sons are bound to repeat what they see. The beginning of a carbon copy.

Although, there are many parents doing the best they can in raising their children to be upright with morals and values. Many children carry on the responsibilities for the severe pain and torment that their parents endured. Many Akers just don't see a way out of breaking the vicious cycle, instead they prefer to inflict pain upon their victims or loved ones. You decide what to call them.

Nevertheless, someone forgot to tell them about the fakers, breakers and takers that are out there lurking around trying to find someone like you or anyone that is vulnerable enough to get caught up in the games that people play.

It is time for us to wake up to the fakers, breakers, and takers' manipulating schemes. Many of us know what an aker really looks like when we see our friends and loved ones going through emotional and psychological rollercoasters, but when we are on the other end of the Aker's schemes, we just 'chalk it up' as love. If love causes that much pain then what does pain *really* feels like? If a faker, breaker, or taker can't find love within themselves then how are they going to love you? Reality check my friends…you cannot help them feel what is not there.

Many women as well as men have had enough time maturing into oneself eager to find out who they are and what's their purpose in life. Going through soul-searching, role-playing, and mind-boggling torture just to find a sense of belonging in today's world. But if each of us had sought after God before running into a faker, a breaker, or a taker we would have probably said, "*if we knew then what we know*

now we could have given ourselves to the Lord a long time ago." There wouldn't have been any distractions leaving you walking into the aker's den. Jesus loves us all in spite of our faults, mistakes, and hang-ups. He is the one Father who loves us unconditionally for the bad and ugly things that we have done. He picks us up and carries us when we think we're all alone.

No one, through all that pain and sorrow, would sacrifice their life for you. Only our Lord and Savior who loves us so dearly would. He died for you and me. God's desire is to dwell within us for "GOD IS LOVE."

I'm telling a true and real story, ironically still going on in the nation now. Many have been through it, Some are still stuck in it, while others just don't know how to get from under or out of it. See women. We're not the only ones going through hard times, our ups and downs, ins, and outs. We just need to recognize that many of our men are TOO!.

Listen, my brothers, I just want to shed some light on this point of view that we understand and can relate with you. However, in order to get past that pain and suffering, we need to come out of the closet and speak out in public.

"Helping others is an encouraging thing to do." It will also help with the healing for all who are going through. It's time to confront the faker, the breakers, and the takers and stop holding back your subjective emotions, public fears, and humiliation. In doing so, you will realize that you are not to blame. We need to stop letting the

Akers blame us for the problems that they're facing.

The abuse keeps coming and the misery won't stop, but if we're to ever escape the oppression from an Aker whether it be emotional, physical, verbal, or sexual, we need to come to terms with the fakers, the breakers, and the takers.

Begin fighting through your darkness and stop letting the devil win. When you feel no way out, go to (Isaiah 40:31). *And know that they who wait upon the Lord shall renew their strength; they shall mount up with wings as eagles, they shall run and not be weary, and they shall walk and not faint.*

Many have been so severely abused in one way or another that they are afraid to get out. The only thing that they can ask is *why did the Caged Bird really sing*? (Maya Angelou) and why are they being trapped in a cage by someone they love, trust, and fantasized about many times before? Many people have trapped themselves in situations of a faker, breaker, and taker's pain because they haven't learned how to fly. It's funny how life's fantasies will wake you up from those falling dreams, into the reality of losing your ability and believing that things in your life are not great. So, are these falling dreams or encountering dreams?

So, check, and inquire about it all. If you set your hopes and dreams of a faker, breaker, and taker's view. You're bound to be undoubtedly confused. They will have you believe the reasons for your pain is your own fault.

Some are so consumed with being in love with a faker,

breaker, and taker that they can't even tell the difference between being in love or living in hell if this is to their advantage or disadvantage or another one of Life disasters.

If only we had taken the time to check the background of a faker, breaker, and taker and find out the issue(s) that they have within. Maybe many of us wouldn't have lost our self-respect, before giving away our hearts, minds, and souls.

Only to find out that everything we see and meet is not pleasing to the eye or good enough to keep. Soon doors start opening and masks begin to peel back, revealing the real joker behind the disguise. Nevertheless, we need to stand back and examine the package that comes across our path. So we can recognize the Aker that comes with them. You see, garbage doesn't start to smell until you leave it around for days in and days out. So be very careful when you are running into a faker, breaker, or taker, for everything about them is built on lies period. An Aker would give you a big picture of a fairy tale life. The only thing about this scenario is that you are wide awake looking at the whole thing transpire in full action. Saying to yourself. " I know he or she really loves me."

They will continue to whisper sweet nothings into your ear while latching onto the things that they want, stop and listen to the words, my friend. Sweet nothings are just what they are telling you… NOTHING! Nothing is sweet about someone taking you for a ride. Many of us get caught up in a relationship like this because we are searching for love. Questionable minds would like to know is it really cheaper to keep them or not? What price would you pay to keep a Faker, Breaker, or Taker?

See an Aker comes in all kinds of disguises and you need to be aware because an Aker would use you for his gain or her come up. When you meet someone for the first time, you don't imagine that person is going to be an Aker in your life. Before you know it, you're losing focus of who you are! Trying to figure out why you are allowing this one individual to take up all your energy....

You must start investigating this person by doing a background check on the person you are about to share your life with. You don't want to come across a Faker, Breaker, or Taker just to end up with an Aker.... For I have dealt with a Breaker and a Taker in my lifetime.

NOW I'M FREE! NO MORE CHAINS HOLDING ME.....

A *FAKER'S* primary goal is to leave you covered with a plethora of physical and emotional scars.

A *BREAKER* will continue to break your heart and will apologize every time since they know that they can get away with it.

A *TAKER* will cut your face so badly that no man whatsoever would want you! Now you're known as DAMAGED GOODS.

An *AKER* will beat you to a pulp if not, maybe kill you! You never know the mindset of an AKER!?!

The Cycle

Carla, Tori, and Terrance had to experience the abuse of living and dealing with an aker in their family. Their biggest struggle was finding a way out, and not letting the cycle begin a generation curse. They have to stand strong and not get trapped into the game of a Faker, Breaker, or Taker. Just to come across an Aker for life.

Serina Garland

Terrance

~THE FAKER~

I came home to the lights out.

"What's going on Mama?"

"I forgot to pay the bill." I was hurt because she gave Ray the light bill money which he didn't pay it.

"Hey baby boy. It's all good! We can have dinner over candlelight," she chuckled.

I grew up an only child and did everything to gain my mother's love and affection only to be ignored again and again. My mother love herself some Ray and he came first. She would do any and everything to please him. I never had an opportunity to know my birth father because he broke up with my Mama before I was born. She never wanted to talk about him to me but she admitted that the only good thing my father gave her was me.

The only thing that my Mama could give me was a picture and his full name. Well with JR added of course. The only thing Mama did tell me was that my dad really did hurt her. In return, it left her angry and bitter. Whenever I would ask Mama to tell me more about my dad, she got upset and told me that she didn't want to think about him.

Ray came home high as usual. Nervously, Mama tried to cover it up by laughing it off.

"Hey Baby, what's up?" My stare was cold as I puzzledly looked over at my Mama.

"What's up?! The damn lights are cut off. That's what's

up!" I screamed out.

"Mama, you got this nigga here who can't help you with a thing!?" Terrance was vexed to say the least.

That thought rolled around in my head for a few minutes before turning back to my Mama.

"Mama, why is he even here? He can't even put the lights back on?" Ray looked up from his glass.

"Boy shut up! I'm the man around here and I'll take care of it tomorrow!" I gave Ray a dirty look that made him jump up from out of his chair yelling at me.

"Boy! I said I'll take care of it and I don't want to hear another damn thing out of your mouth!" I yelled back!

"Man, my name is Terrance to you!" I got up and excused myself to my room. Soon as I closed the door, I heard my Mama yelling at Ray about the light bill money. Once again he gave her a lame ass excuse about how he had to use it. He said he will pay the bill for her tomorrow.

"You used it for what Ray?" Her tone confirmed that Ray once again manipulated Mama.

"Baby!" he started his game in full throttle. "I *said* I'll pay the bill tomorrow and the lights will be turned back on!" He yelled. My Mama didn't even argue. She just said '*ok*'.

When I got up for school the next morning, Mama had already left for work. Ray was on the phone talking with somebody about coming to get something. But once he noticed that I was standing there, he looked frighten and jumped up.

"Man, make yourself known when you enter a room."

"Why? You have something to hide?" I was ready for war although I knew Ray could break my bones but I didn't care.

"You and that mouth of yours boy is going to cause you to write a check..."

"That *you* can't cash," I respond cutting him off in midsentence as I was slowly walking out of the house. Ray looked at me with eyes that could kill.

"Boy, get out my face!" He continued with his phone call. I just don't understand how many times my mother is going to let men walk all over her. She just hasn't been one to pick a good man. So many of them lie to her. Taking her on roller coaster rides that keeps her so dizzy she can't even see the bullshit that they are pushing, let alone they don't mean her any good.

When I got back home from school. Ray was still at home now entertaining his friends. I yelled out for my mother.

"Boy stop yelling in this damn house. Your Mama's not here," he said. There were beer cans lying all over the place. Cocaine sat out in open display on the table. Ray tried to cover it up by placing a lamp shade on it, but I had saw it already. I often wondered if Ray even had a job. I was angered to say the least as I looked over at Ray in hatred.

"What's up boy?" I shook my head and continued to my room. As I was taking my shirt off, the thoughts in my head were telling me something's wrong about this dude. I just can't put my finger on...yet. As I went to flip the light switch up, nothing happened. They were still off. I was heated! I began shouting at him from my bedroom.

"What happened to you putting the lights back on man!? Why haven't you paid the fucking bill yet!?" Ray came tumbling down the hall like a running back.

"I said I paid that shit kid! The damn light company didn't turn them back on yet! And next time, you better watch that bass in your voice when you talking to me!" His stance made me feel uncomfortable.

"Oh my! Look at you growing those little chest hairs." It wasn't his sarcasm that bothered me. It was more so the way he said it that made me feel very unease. Has he been looking at me sideways the whole time?

When my Mama got home Ray and his friends had already split, leaving her to clean up all of their mess. I came from out of my room when I heard her fussing about it. Once she saw me, she asked what was this all about?

"Wait Mama. This is not my mess. You already know whose mess this is. It was your man and his buddies' mess."

She flipped on the lights switch only to find nothing

happened.

"Shit, the lights still are not on," she said aloud as she sat down and began to cry. I told her that Ray is not the guy for her and that she can do better.

"That's enough T. I got this," she hurtfully uttered.

"Mama do you? Because Ray has a lot going on. And I think his feelings for you just are not the same. Her eyes became weary.

"T, just go to your room. I had a hard day and don't need this shit right now."

"You should be paying attention, Mama!"

As I was heading down the hall to my room, Ray came back into the house still stumbling all over himself. Mama started blasting off.

"Ray what is this shit all about and why my damn lights are not back on?! Huh? I gave you the money two days ago and you used it for God knows what!" Her anger was an understatement.

"You said you were going to have the lights turned back on today!" Now here comes Ray's master manipulation technique.

"Pat,". I went to the electric company and they said it was going to be turned back on today by 5 o'clock this evening." Deep down, Mama's heart was hurting knowing Ray had spent the light bill money on either drugs, alcohol, or both . But for the life of me,

I couldn't understand why she still puts up with his lies and blatant disrespect to us.

"Ok Ray, but it's well after five O'clock Now. Why the fuck my lights are not back on yet, huh?" Ray's body was wreaking of alcohol.

"Woman, I don't know what those people are doing!" he snapped back as if it was her fault the lights are not back on.

Mama looked at him then rolled her eyes. "What the hell is all this mess Raymond?" Ray looked at my mother and spoke nonchalantly.

"Woman, calm down. I got this," he said trying to stand tall but the alcohol has the best of him. Mama looked at Ray and told him to clean this mess up.

"Ok, *Mama*, ok." He said sarcastically.

"Ray, my house is not a place to entertain your friends that supposed to be working like you."

"What are you talking about Pat? First I thought this was *our* house. I didn't know I needed permission to have people over."

"You're not leaving me with this mess to clean up Ray." Ray grabbed onto each of my mama's arms pulling her close to him and began kissing all over her. Touching her in places that I did not need to see. So, I just headed back to my room.

Suddenly, it became eerily quiet that I left from out of my

bedroom to see if things were ok. Mama and Ray were in her bedroom. Then she let out a howling laugh. I guess Ray won again. When I got up the next morning, Ray had left and mama was cleaning up.

"Where's Ray?"

"He said he had something to do last night."

Wow, I thought to myself. So, Ray did not even stay here with mama last night. Mama called the light company just to find out that Ray never paid the bill of $439.00. She had to pay the entire amount in order to get the electricity turned back on. She had given Ray $450.00 and he didn't even bring her the change back. Mama had to pay out more money that she didn't have.

Mama started crying and saying she can't believe this damn man lied.

"I told you Mama there's something about him that just isn't right."

"Ok T, I don't want to hear that right now." "Why do you allow him to treat you like this?" I asked.

"Ray is wonderful to us baby." I just gazed at her .

"To whom Mama? He's not even nice to you! He lies to you all the time. I never see him take you out anywhere! And what bills does he pay?"

"T, why would you say things like that. Ray tries very hard to like you."

"It's not about liking me Mama. It's about having respect for you."

"Baby, please give him a chance," she begged.

"Why Mama!? He left you to pay the light bill that he said he paid already. You shouldn't have given him any money."

Terrance continued, "He as your man should of have paid it for you. I might be young but I'm not dumb. I see that Ray is not right for you Mama." I couldn't get that concept through to her so I told her I got to go to school. I couldn't stand to hear her defending Ray any longer.

As I was on my way to school, I couldn't wait to see my friend Tori. She seemed to be a good listener. Tori and I were happy to see one another again; greeting each other with a hug and a big smile, happy that we could talk again.

We found it easy to identify with the things that each of us are going through. We seem to have a lot in common which is how we became real good friends in such a short time. They both were happy that they became friends because neither haven't had a good friend in such a long time.

Tori stayed to herself. Her home and family life were too much for her to deal with, let alone explaining and repeating her feelings and problems to others. Terrance felt the same way which is why he too walked alone. Tori asked Terrance how he was doing since their last conversation. Terrance began telling

Tori about the things that he was so depressed about.

"My Mama is my biggest concern. Don't get me wrong. She's a good woman. It's just that she has poor taste in who she picks as her man...or whatever they are to her." Tori felt sorry for her friend. Terrance continued.

"My Mama always seems to get played by them, but she doesn't see that. She takes in all these stray cats that don't care about her, and this hurts because I have to see it all." Terrance paused before continuing again.

"Tori, my Mama is all I have and she's my Queen! She's a hardworking single mom and I'm so blessed to have her. But Tori I'm afraid."

Tori looked at him. "Afraid of what Terrance?"

"I'm afraid at the length that I would go to protect her. She's the only family I have. I'm trying so hard to finish high school and get a good paying job to support myself and get my own so I can move my Mama away from here. She needs to see that she can make it on her own. Damn it, she's doing it now." I really need to get from under this mess at home.

"So, Terrance if I might ask, where is your dad?" Stunned by her razor-sharp question, Terrance looked up at Tori with such unhappiness in his eyes.

"Tori, I don't know," he said quietly. "I never got the chance to meet him. My Mama would only just say that I was named after him and I was the best and only good gift that he's ever given her. She has one other sibling but I never met her, and she don't talk about her to me, either"

"So, what's your goal Terrance?" Tori asked. "Well, I would love to be a dental hygienist." Tori smile.

"Oh ok. I see. Is that why you have those perfect white teeth." They both laughed. Terrance and Tori were so interested in finding out about each other that they ended up on the football field. They sat down at the bleachers to finish talking. Tori found a relief in talking to Terrance. He was a good listener as well. They were so engrossed into each other's stories, they never noticed Carla sitting a few seats up crying. When Tori looked up, she saw Carla and tapped Terrance to show him that something was wrong with that girl. Terrance as compassionate as he is, started up the bleachers.

"Hello, I'm not trying to be nosey, but I just wanted to know if you were alright. Carla looked up and was so surprised that this handsome guy was speaking to her. She caught Tori smiling up at them.

"Yes, I'm good," she replied softly

"Ok. I hope you feel better," Terrance said then started back down the bleachers.

"So, Tori," he said. "What's up with you? What's the story behind the sadness in your eyes?"

"What do you mean?"

"I see the expression on your face when I speak on the things that I'm dealing with. How's home life treating you?"

"As I listen to you Terrance," she began sadly, "it's like you are telling some of my story. I don't know my dad either, my Mama doesn't speak to her family." I stop for a short time staring at his handsome face. He sure was a sight to see. I didn't want him to think bad about me, especially since we just met. I continued to tell him my story.

"I have an 8-year-old brother and a 1-year-old sister, and a mother who believed everything her man said. She's all caught up with my sister's father, Victor, who's a piece of caca to put it nicely!" They both laughed.

"Victor can never do any wrong in my mama's eyes. He just takes and takes from her. I have yet to see him support her at all."

As she began to go deeper into her life problems at home, she noticed Carla began crying harder. Ironically, they both had looked at each other at the same time.

"Are you ok?" They both asked.

"Do you need help with something?" Tori asked out of concern. Carla shrugged her shoulders.

"Where do I begin?" Her tears started rolling down even faster.

"There's so much going on in my life. I don't know where

to begin. I'm only 15. I'm not supposed to be dealing with these types of problems. I can't seem to get a grip on my own situations in life. How can I help someone else when I don't even understand what it is that I'm going through?" Carla realized she was getting ready to tell strangers about things that was happening in her life, yet she didn't even know them. She had to stop and apologize for crying so loud and interrupting them in their own conversation.

"I don't have no room to put my problems on you guys. Forgive me. Go on with what you were doing." Tori got up and introduce herself and said to Carla with every ounce of compassion,

"Please, It's ok. I think we're going through some type of hardships in our young lives that we should not be handling by ourselves."

Carla stopped crying and they all started to talk to one another. Carla looked at them both and said that she was glad that she met them because she was feeling so lonely.

"The things I'm going through is my secret and mine's alone."

"You are not alone Carla," Tori followed suit.

"You sure aren't. We have our own family secrets to figure out too." They all decided that they will stay friends and have each other's back. They continued to talk for a long time until Carla suddenly realized that it was getting late. Both Terrance and Tori said yes it is then they all jumped up to leave.

"Let's meet back here again tomorrow," I stated. Tori said she would like that and Carla agreed.

When I arrived home, the lights were back on but there was no Mama or Ray. I was chilling in the living room watching TV when the door opened and in comes Mama and Ray, both laughing. She was acting just like this character didn't just throw her under the bus.

"Hey T," said Mama.

"What's up mama?" I replied back. Then Ray had the audacity to ask me *what up dude*!? I gave him a dirty look.

"Man, my name is Terrance."

"Yeah, Yeah, Whatever." Then looked at me and laughed .

That made me ask Mama what's up again? She shot me a look. "

"T. Not now." Ray grabbed her and took her into the bedroom and that was that. I didn't see Mama till the next morning.

I was really feeling some type of way this morning. I kept wondering why Mama never told me the story about my dad. My mind was racing with so many questions and it was time for Mama to tell me the story. I was at the age where I was curious in wanting to know why he left me.

Mama was all smiles when I walked in.

"Hey baby. I'm making breakfast. What would you like?"

"I just want some answers Mama. You know…about my donor." No sooner than I said that Ray came strolling into the kitchen.

"What are you two in here talking about?" I peered at mama like she better not say anything to this cat!

Mama snickered. "My baby got questions for me."

"About what?" Ray asked.

"Nunya!" I replied angrily.

"Nunya? Ray asked puzzledly.

"I said yes, none of your damn business!"

Mama yelled. "T, apologize to Ray. That's not how you speak to an adult." I was boiling in anger.

" Mama what!? He's not someone I can respect.   Look at how he treats you!"

"T, Stop! Stop now!" Mama yelled out furiously. Ray jumped up, to come at me then Mama hollered,

"Ray! No!" Ray looked at Mama spitting fire out.

"Fuck this shit! I'm out!" Mama ran behind Ray.

"Baby, wait! It's ok. Come on baby lets go in the room," she pleaded sounding so pitiful. Ray then went into the room with her.

"Mama, I'm not finished talking," I said enraged.

"T, not right now," She continued cautiously to her room with Ray following along. I could hear her giggling and saying stop Ray. I knew that was my cue to leave. Today is Friday and I'm feeling very depressed. School was my great escape. Some kids couldn't wait for Friday, but not me. I dreaded it because I knew I was going to have to see and deal with Ray being at the house this weekend.

When I got to school, I couldn't wait to run into Tori and Carla. Talking to them made my day a lot better. Not because they have problems as well, just because we can relate to each other. It was so funny how we all been going to the same school and didn't even know one another or had any classes together. I was into just learning all about being a good Orthodontic, so that I could be the best. As I was sitting in the cafeteria reading a book on dentistry, I was so deep in thought that I didn't even notice the girls coming up to me.

"Hello Terrance!" Tori said in excitement. She noticed right off the back that something was bothering me.

"What's wrong Terrance? Where's that great smile of yours?" Tori asked. Carla looked over at him as well.

"What's going on Terrance?" Carla said caringly.

"Whatever it is, shake it off and remember there is nothing that we as friends can't talk about or deal with," Carla said. Tori decided that we should call ourselves the C.T.T. which stand for (Can't Touch This). We all like the title of it. Tori said it means that we won't let other people's problems affect our outcomes and we will release our emotions so that it will not touch our hearts. Let's not fall into their cycle but break it. They all said 'yes' simultaneously. We liked it. That's what the CTT guys will do and we will follow and agree to the terms. CTT stands for us all. Carla, Terrance, and Tori.

I began to tell them about my morning. And how my Mama took Ray side and left me in the kitchen without even given me the chance to find out anything about my dad.

"I can relate to what you are saying Terrance because my mother hasn't told me why my dad isn't in my life either," Tori continued.

"Every time I asked her, she changed the subject."

Carla chimed in. "Terrance, why you can't find your dad? So that way you can ask him these questions. Do you know any of his information?"

"I just know his name," I said.

"Then let's make this a task for us all and at the same time let's find out information about your dad Tori."

"Yes. If I can get anything out of my Mama," I said.

"I sure would like to know why my dad just left me and why he didn't want to know anything about me. The search is on."

I began telling the girls how I dread that today is

Friday.

"Why?" Carla asked.

"Because I have to deal with being in that house with Ray. It's not like I have a bunch of "*homeboys*" that I can hang out with.

Tori then chimed in. "Why don't you guys come over and we can do the search at my house."

I was relieved to get the invitation. That put a big smile on my face. Tori noticed my face light up.

"Now, that's the smile I like to see plus those big pretty pearly whites." I blushed while still trying to keep up my swag. But now Carla was starting to feel some kind of way.

"Carla what's wrong?" Tori asked.

"Well, you know my Aunt Mimi is not going to let me go anywhere."

"Why?" I asked.

"Well, because I'm the babysitter, while she plays and do her thing with Tyrone. Tyrone has my Aunt Mimi doing all kinds of things on the weekend, like selling her body, stealing from stores, just to supply him with drugs. She doesn't even care what could happen to her, let alone us.

"Well! just bring them with you to my house, my mother won't mind. They can play with Joseph and Sophie. (Carla sighs at the thought). Ok she said I'll see. So, the CTT went back to their next class, after getting each other's address. Finding out that they didn't even live that far from each other.

When I got home, my Mama was actually there and sitting in the kitchen with Ray drinking with some of his guy friends. No couple's, just Mama. I was surprised to see her a little tipsy. I never seen that side of my Mama before. She jumped up to greet me.

"Baby, I'm so sorry about dis morning. I love you." She said while hugging and kissing me.

"It's ok Mama," I hugged her back. Then, of course, Ray jumped in with his unneeded comment.

"Woman! Come on and leave that boy alone." I didn't say a word. I just went to my room. I didn't want to upset my Mama's night. I never get the chance to see her relax. I just put my headset on to tune out the music and loud noise.

After a while I went into the kitchen to get something to eat and drink. I noticed my Mama was on the couch passed out. I didn't see Ray anywhere as I went to put a hot pocket in the microwave. Afterwards, I headed to the bathroom and just as I was about to open the door I heard a man voice.

"Yes, man right there," I heard Ray ask does that feel good?" I stood there for a moment listening to what was going to happen next. Finally, I banged on the door and said I have to use the bathroom. Ray finally opened it with a stupid look on his face.

"This man done burn the shit out his hand and I had to put something on it." He turned around to his friend who was covering up his hand.

"Yeah man that feels better." I just looked at Ray and shook my head. I went back to the living room to wake my Mama up.

"She's good man."

"No, she's not. Mama! Wake up and go into the bedroom. You're tired." I then helped her to the room and yelled at Ray's friends to leave. It shocked me that Ray did not fight with me on this. Instead, he agreed. I looked at him in bewilderment because he never agreed on anything I said before. *Why now? Ummm?* He couldn't even look at me in the face. He just left with his friends.

I sat in the living room trying to make sense out of what I just heard in the bathroom between him and his friend and wondered, if his friend's hand was really burned or not. He had it covered so I couldn't tell. I shook it off and was relieved that they left and my Mama was safe in her room.

The next morning, I prepared to go to Tori house to search for my dad. I check to see if my Mama was ok before I left.

"What made you drink like that last night, Mama?"

"Terrance, I was just trying to relax. What's wrong with that?"

"It's nothing wrong with it Mama but you have to be alert at all times.

"Why T. What happened?"

"Nothing Mama. I'm just saying."

"How much do you know about Ray?"

"I know I love him T. Why? What's up with all these questions?"

"Nothing Mama just be careful please." I then left to go to Tori's house.

We all had a great time just chatting with each other and watching the kids have fun. Our search was getting us nowhere. Carla decided to widen the search and go to Ancestors.com. As we were about to surf the internet, Tori's Mama came in bleeding all over her face. She was so embarrassed when she saw us, she quickly ran to the bathroom.

Carla and I knew that was our cue to leave. The girls were having so much fun and didn't want to go, but I told them that we need to get back home. We both said our goodbyes to Tori and we let her know we really enjoyed our time we shared today.

"Thanks. Let's do this again...soon." Tori's voice was full of misery.

When I got back home, Mama was laying on the couch. I asked her was she ok.

Slowly, she looked at me.

"Yes baby I'm fine." Ray came in minutes after me and asked my Mama to get up and make him something to eat. Mama said she was not feeling up to it today. But Ray refused to see that she was just trying to relax.

"This cat only thinks about himself." I glanced over at my Mama.

"You look a little under the weather, Mama. Let me help you to your room so you can lay down in your bed. I'll bring you some Tylenol." Ray looked at me with a stare of death.

"Boy! I just told her to get me something to eat!"

"Get it yourself can't you see that she's not feeling well."

I shot back.

"Man, that woman is fine!" Ray barked.

"Not today she's not!" Then Ray had the audacity to grab my mother. He seen the razor-sharp gaze on my face. He stopped dead in his tracks looking at me with a venomous hate. Then paused.

"Boy, I can't with you today." Strangely enough, he just left out of the door. I knew mama was sick because she didn't take the time to defend Ray. That night Ray did not come back nor did he even call to check up on my mother.

The next morning which was Sunday Mama stayed in the bed and I took care of her. There was No Ray! And I was relieved. I always let Mama take care of me. Now it was my turn to look after her. I went into the kitchen to make her some soup and I found something else instead. It was a syringe. I'm guessing it's used for drugs since no one in here is insulin dependent.

"That damn Ray!" I mumbled because I knew it wasn't Mama's. I didn't tell her what I found because that would have just made her feel even worst and plus worried. I continued fixing her soup and took it to her. Mama sat up and was coughing all over the place.

"T, my whole body hurts." I could see the pain in her face.

"I know Mama. You really don't look too good." She nodded in agreement. "We need to make you a doctor's appointment."

"I will, baby. Just let me rest please. Maybe I drunk a little too much and just having a hangover," she chuckled.

I slept in the living room so I could hear her if she called me. Another night without Ray and no phone call either. Funny how he's *so* in love with mama until she gets sick.

Monday morning snuck in and Mama still wasn't feeling good. I accompanied her to the doctor. The doctor told her that it sounds like the flu.

"Let's get some blood work done on you," he said as he was preparing her a note to be out of work for a few days. They will have her results in a few days.

After we returned home, Mama went to lay on the couch

and I went into the kitchen to prepare her something to eat. Then all of a sudden, who comes in? Ray! He looked over at Mama.

"Are you still sick woman?" Mama sent him a mean stare.

"Yes, Ray and where have you been? When I needed you, you were nowhere to be found!"

"Hey woman. I didn't come here to hear all your shit. It didn't make no sense in both of us being sick. But how the hell are you feeling now?"

"I'm feeling a little better, Bae." Ray sat down beside mama and started kissing all over her. I was so disgusted at the thought of him touching my mother. *How selfish of this man.*

Weeks went by and Mama started feeling a little better. I didn't get to see the girls for about a week now. We all seem to be going in our own directions. We're going to be juniors this year and our main focus was trying to make it through for our senior year. I've been trying hard to be strong for my Mama, especially since she has been sick lately.

I got a job to help Mama with the bills. Ray was just in the way and nevered help Mama with anything but he always had his hands out for her to give him something. Since Mama has been sick, Ray has shown no concern for her or her health. Yet he continued bringing his friends to the house knowing that mama was ill.

Mama spent most of her time lying in the bed when she

came home from work. I knew she was still feeling under the weather and needed her rest afterwards. Ray spent all of his time entertaining his friends. One day I walked into the living room and two of Ray's friends kissing on each other. I stopped in my tracks.

"What the hell is going on in here?!" I screamed out. Ray turned around to see what I was talking about and tried to play like he didn't know what they were doing by yelling at them.

"What the heck are you two doing over there?" Like he didn't know.

"You two have to get the hell out of here with that mess because this shit is not going down like that in here!" I angrily shouted.

"Go get a room or something. I could care less. Just leave my mama house now."

Ray looked at me. "Boy you don't have no right to tell nobody to get out of *my* house. I will be the one to do that! I am the boss in this house when your mama not around."

I looked at him with a wicked facial expression.

"Look man, I had enough of your shit. You're not paying one damn bill in this house. So, you don't have no room to give me orders!"

Ray continued to yell. "Boy take your ass to your room and shut up with all that bullshit!" No sooner than he said that Mama came out of her room shouting.

"What is going on?!"

"Woman, you better get your damn son before I have to teach him how to respect his elders!" Mama looked at Ray.

"Hold up! What the hell is going on in here?!" She was baffled to say the least.

"What do it look like woman?"

"I'm entertaining my company. That's what's going on!"

"Well, I'm not feeling good! So, you have to entertain your friends somewhere else." My Mama shocked me. She never yells back at Ray let alone defend me to him. Ray then smoothly walked over to Mama hugging and kissing on her neck.

"Come on woman. Don't get your panties in a bunch. I'll take care of the guys." Mama pushed Ray off of her.

"...and I prefer you leave as well! I just want to be alone right now." Ray couldn't believe his ears then look at Mama shrugged his shoulders, and shook his head. He then mumbled,

"I can't believe this shit." He then followed suit after his riffraff. I was so relieved. At that moment, I knew that Mama really wasn't feeling well. When she dismissed Ray I knew she was feeling as bad as she looked.

"Mama, just go back to bed. I will bring you something to eat." She wasn't look good at all.

"I'm ok T. I just can't seem to shake this flu." Two weeks

has passed by and mama still wasn't feeling quite herself. She didn't seem to be in the mood for Ray either. Since Mama has been sick, I got a job at the warehouse stacking boxes. This paid a pretty good paycheck and I was able to help Mama pay the bills, while she was out of work. This meant that I really didn't have time to talk to the girls. They would call me on the phone to see if I had time to see them and chat because I was either at work or trying to get home to Mama. During those two weeks, we didn't see Ray. Mama was so sick that Ray was the furthest thing from her mind.

I came home from school one day to find Ray at the house. When I open the door and seen him my whole attitude changed.

"What the hell are you doing here?" Mama was sitting on the couch looking at Ray with a disgusted look on her face. I looked at Mama to see if she was going to correct me. She turned to Ray,

"It's time for you to leave." Ray was puzzled. He looked over at Mama.

"What are you talking about baby? Oh, you don't want me here anymore?" My Mama's response was even more sinister than Ray's games he's been playing.

"Ray, just get the fuck out of my house and I don't want to see your ass again!" Ray jumped up and looked at my Mama.

"What are you talking about woman? What's this all about and who are you talking to?" Mama yelled!

"I'm talking to you MUH FUCKA! Now get the fuck out of my house!" Ray looked at my Mama like he was about to hit her. Immediately, I jumped up.

"Oh, hell no! She said, get the fuck out of her house!"

"Boy, if you don't get out of my face," he yelled. "Go ahead! Give me a reason to whip your ass, boy!"

Mama jumped up off of the couch in lightning-fast speed.

"You're not putting your nasty ass hands on my son. Now get out of my house!" Ray hurried up and left.

Once he was gone, I asked mama what was that all about?

"You just put *your* man out."

"Humph, you mean somebody else's man," Mama said under her breath.

"Huh? What was that Mama?" I asked with my ear facing her.

"Nothing son. Nothing. "

After I got Mama settled in for the night, I was trying to understand what just happened. What made Mama say all of those things to Ray? I was glad that she did, but I wanted to know what was it all for?

Several weeks passed by and Mama still didn't go to

work. I looked at her and quickly realized something different about her. My Mama had been losing a lot of weight. I ask my mother was she ok since she has not been back to work in over a month and it doesn't seem like this flu was getting any better.

"Mama you look like you losing weight. What's the doctor saying about your blood work? Mama began to cry.

"T, I just can't talk about it right now baby. I have to figure this one out for myself."

"Mama, all we have is each other to lean on and you have to understand that I am not a little boy anymore. I'm a young man who's been holding us down. Just talk to me Mama," I begged.

"I will T. Just not right now! Just let Mama be alone baby, please?"

I left her to roam around in her own thoughts while I ran around in mines. I had to get another job to keep us from getting evicted because Mama was still sick. She was not in any shape to work right now. So, I needed to step up and be that man she taught me to be. I got another job at the food court to help with other bills around the house. I was so glad that school was about to end for the summer. I could take in more hours. I haven't had a chance to talk to the ladies. My mind haven't been on anything else except just trying to work out my own problems. I want to keep Mama and me above water. I went to work and worried about her all day. I just couldn't shake the thought of Mama not getting better.

When I got home, Mama was laid out on the floor, she was not moving. I ran over to see if she was still breathing. Thank God she was. I called the ambulance and they arrived quickly taking Mama to the hospital.

I rode with her in the back of the ambulance. Mama started moving.

"Mama, what happened?" I said grabbing hold of her fragile hands.

"I got dizzy and I must've I passed out." When we got to the emergency room they took Mama in the back and told me that someone will come out to talk to me. It seemed like I was in the emergency room for hours. Finally, a doctor came out to tell me that my Mama was very sick and she needs to be admitted.

"What's wrong with my mother?" I asked the doctor. He said that he could not discuss my mother's medical condition with me. He then gave me her room number and told me to give the nurses a few minutes and then I could go up to see her.

When I got to my Mama's room, she was resting. I quietly entered then kissed her on the forehead which woke her up.

"Hey baby. I'm so sorry if I scared you. I was trying to do somethings for myself before you got home. Next thing I knew, I couldn't breathe." I looked at my Mama with the feeling of concern.

Serina Garland

"What's going on, Mama? What is the doctor saying about your health?" Mama just looked at Me with tears forming in the webs of her eyes. Chills started slithering down my spine.

"Son, I'll be alright," she groggily said.

"Mama, please tell me what's wrong with you? Why are we here? Did they say it was cancer?"

"No Baby! They didn't say that at all. Go home and relax. I will be fine." She tried to convince me that she was fine but I know something was seriously wrong.

"Mama, how am I supposed to relax when you are here in the hospital?"

"I will be home tomorrow...hopefully," she softly said.

I looked at my mother with so much concern in my eyes, and just nodded my head. I gave her a kiss and left. I really couldn't wait to get home because I was very tired. I had a long day at work. My body was there but my mind was on my Mama.

Once I got home, I started cleaning up the mess that she made. I went into her room to put things back in its place. I noticed a lot of pills in her nightstand. I was curious to see what kind of medicine my Mama was taking. I read the bottles. I didn't understand the name of the medications or what they were for. So, I wrote the names of some of the medication down...*Ziagen, Emtriva, and Prednisolone* so I could check them out later.

I called Mama's room to see if she was going to be

discharged today. She told me that they want to run some more tests on her so she won't be coming home today.

"What have they told you?" I asked.

"Baby, the doctors haven't said anything to me yet. When they do baby, I will let you know. Don't worry baby." She paused.

"Mama will be alright." Truthfully, she knew whatever news she receives from the doctor was going to be bad. The doctor just came in the room baby. I'll call you right back."

****

PATRICIA

Finally, the doctor came in. The expression on his face had me scared.

"Ms. Freeman," he began then taking a deep sigh.

"Your tests results showed that your CD4 count has fallen below 200 cells per cubic millimeter and your viral load is dangerously high which is an indication that you HIV virus has developed into AIDS and its now aggressive. There is nothing we can do. It's coming on fast."

"Wait. What!" Nooo! Nooo!" My mind was now in a ball of confusion. "My son needs me. I need him. How in the hell did I get this? When did I get this? How long...?!" Questions were shooting right and left from my mouth.

"What am I supposed to do? Huh? Tell me what am I supposed to do?!" I couldn't stop my tears raging down my face. I was frantic. My mind finally went mute until I snapped back into reality. "OMG! I got AIDS? What am I supposed to tell my son? My only child!" I was in a state of disbelief.

The doctor looked at me trying to reassure me that they would do all that they can to help keep me comfortable, but he strongly advised me that I need to get my affairs in order.

****

I went to work at the food court and ran into Carla. I was happy to see her because we haven't seen each other in a while. I wanted to sit down and chat with her and let her know what's been going on with me.

"Have you talked to Tori?" I asked.

"No. I haven't talked to her since the last time we were at her house."

"That's about how long it's been since I last talk to her, too. I hope everything is ok with her and that she's doing good."

"Carla, you will not believe what I've been through. We have to catch up but I'm working and my lunch break is almost over. I have to go back to work. I can't afford to lose this job. I'll connect with you soon. Is your number still the same?"

"Yes."

"Is yours still the same? Of course," I replied smiling.

"Ok. We will hook back up soon." Carla returned the smile back.

Later that day, I spotted Ray at the food court with a couple of his friends, but he didn't notice me looking at him. All I could do was think back to the last time he was at the house how my Mama grew mental strength and kicked him out. In the back of my head, I still was in disbelief of her doing that. I was so busy watching Ray.

Soon after, my curiosity wanted to know why he was so

close and personal with the man beside him. Ray's arm was wrapped around his shoulders acting just like that guy was his boo or something. Like they were straight up couples. As I watched even more at the guy Ray was hugged up on, I noticed that that was the same guy from the bathroom.

"Terrance!" I jumped in my tracks when I heard someone shouting out my name. It was my manager telling me to get back to work. I was so relieved that Ray didn't come over to my station.

As I was getting off the clock, my phone rung. It was my mother on the other end.

"Hi baby. They will be releasing me in the morning."

"Ok. I will let my boss know and be there to get you in the morning."

When I got to the hospital my Mama was ready to go. I noticed her eyes were blood shot red. I could tell she'd been crying hard. I just don't know about what. For some reason, I became scared.

"Mama, is everything alright?" She just dropped her head. I was glad that her discharging process didn't take too long. We got back home and Mama told me that she wanted to talk about something.

"Ok, Mama about what? What's going on?"

"Well baby let us get settled then we'll talk."

"I finished everything I had to do. I made sure that my

Mama bedroom was in order for her."

"Do you want to lay down?"

"Not right now, T. Come sit by me for a while." I sat down beside my Mama. Immediately, she began to cry. I hugged her tight telling her everything will be ok.

"What's wrong? What did the doctor's say Mama?"

"T, it's not just that. I don't want to leave you without me telling you about your, as you call him, donor. I need to tell you about your father." She then took a deep sigh before continuing.

"You know that your Mama love you so much, right?"

"Mama, I know you do."

"You know that you are the joy of my life. Right?!"

"Yes Mama I know!" I was anticipating what she was going to tell me about my donor. I was ready to finally get some closure about this man, that she says is my father.

"Well T, I left your dad because he was sleeping with my sister and got her pregnant as well."

"What! Mama what?! Why?" Nothing could prepare me for what she'd just hit me with.

"T, all I know is that I cut my sister out of my life a long time ago. Your father is a very distance memory to me as well. He hurt me T, he betrayed me in the worse way. He hurt me so much that my heart felt like it was ripped out of my chest and stomped on. It wasn't broken into pieces. It was smashed. I...I couldn't recover from that shit! I was so shattered. I couldn't believe that either one of them would do this to me." Mama blew slowly through her lips before she resumed.

"My sister, T! My very own Sister! She knew how much I loved that man. But that wasn't the part that got me so stressed out. It was the fact that she was two fuckin' months pregnant and she knew that I was three months along. So, I guess this bullshit was going on behind my back for a long time."

All I could do was look at Mama with such sadness and pity.

"What did your mother say?"

"Baby, she told me that I needed to be ashamed of myself."

I looked at Mama puzzledly.

"What are you saying?"

"She had the nerve to say that I knew my sister had him first!"

"What??" Then Mama continued.

"I said Ma, I was the one who introduced you to Terrance, how could you forget that? Are you senile or do you have dementia or something? She told me to leave it alone." She always took my sister's side. Then she had the nerve to tell me that it would work it's self out. I remembered screaming out how, Mama!? We're both pregnant by the same man!"

She didn't want to talk about it anymore and just left me standing there outside as she turned her back on me and went in her house." Tears continued falling down my Mama's face.

"Your dad had the nerve to tell me that he had always wanted to be with my sister and that he had to *follow his heart*. I yelled what the fuck do you mean *your* heart? What the fuck about mines? He said that he loved her and wanted to be with her and their baby. Like I wasn't standing there poked the fuck out. They had the audacity to even set a date to get married. I knew it was time for me to get away from all this bullshit. He even had the nerve to tell me to abort you. I slapped that muthafucka and then I spit in his damn face and walked the hell away."

"He wasn't going to play me or my baby as second fiddle. I left all that toxic shit behind. Your dad never once tried to find you or even wanted to know if I had a girl or a boy." Mama's soul was forever broken and I saw it written all over her face.

"I loved him T. That's why I gave you his name. What they did hurt me! It hurt me so bad, but you were the joy of my life and heart...the one and only thing no one could ever take from me."

Mama gave me a piece of paper with my father's name and address on it.

"This is for you baby, if you want to reach out to your dad."

"I'll think about it," I said while trying to shield my tears from my Mama.

"I can't believe your own sister would do something like that to you."

"Terrance, some people don't care about other people. Instead, they just want what other people have. Never asking just taking. They're only after what they want for themselves. You would think that your family has your back or your best interest at heart, but not mines."

"I'm so sorry T that I kept this from you all this time."

Mama began to cry harder and harder.

"Sorry that this news about your father couldn't have been better news."

I held my Mama trying to console her.

"Mama please stop crying. Please tell me why? Why did he do this to you?"

"T, I don't know why either one of them did what they did. I just had to remove myself and my feelings out of the way. I knew I was having a baby and I didn't want to catch a case and give birth to you in jail. I knew that it was time to let you know. I knew you were going to have questions one day."

"I was devastated when they told me that they were getting married. I couldn't believe what I was hearing. I probably could have taken it a little better if it wasn't my sister! My very own sister. That shit hurt baby, especially finding out that the bitch was having his baby too. I just wanted to get far away from them." As Mama continued venting, I knew that I had to just listen because she'd kept this all in for so many years.

"The day I had you, there was no one there. Until I met D. She really became a good friend. We been friends ever since."

"What happened with you two?

"I let her down when I met that dam Ray. I wish I never did that. But we live and we learn. I just knew that I never wanted to see your dad or my sister again. I guess he thought life with her would be better."

"Mama, why are you telling me this now?"

"I just felt it was time you knew about him and why I only had that one picture of him."

"I hear what you're saying Mama, but why now?"

"I just wanted you to know about your father and get a relationship with him for yourself."

"Mama, you are my family. You have been one strong woman and you have always been here for me. You are *my* Mama and my father. Now that I know the story about my donor, I don't care to meet him or any of our family. I'm good Mama." She gave me a tight hug while apologizing again to me.

"T, I'm tired, baby."

"Ok," I said. "Mama, I'm glad that you open up to me

Serina Garland

about my donor but I still want to know what did the doctor say about your health. For some reason, you keep passing by that question. Why Mama? What's up?"

"I'm going to lay down for a while, baby. I'm tired. We'll talk more later."

"Yes Mama. Ok, you just get you some rest," I replied because I didn't want to over exhaust her.

"I have to go into work tomorrow at 2pm. I will be back at 10 PM. Will you be ok 'til then Mama?"

"Yes baby go to work. I will be fine." I wanted to go back into my Mama's room to talk some more, but she was fast asleep. I still had unanswered questions. I wanted to know why she was so sick and tired lately and what did the doctors tell her about what was going on with her.

I had some time to chill, so I decided to look up the names of the medication that she has been taking. Just as I was about to do that, Tori called.

"How are things going with you?"

"I finally got the information about my donor." Tori was happy to hear that.

"So, tell me what are you going to do next? What else has been going on with you?"

Instead of telling her the truth, I bent the truth.

"I've been good Tori. My Mama hasn't been well lately.

She's been so sick. So, I've been working two jobs to take care of everything."

"Wow."

"Tori, we have to hook up sometime."

"We have to get together with Carla and bring back the CTT," he said.

"I miss you guys so much. I've haven't been doing anything with myself either, Terrance. I've been falling back on my drawing."

"Why's that?

"I've been too busy playing *MOMMA* to my siblings. Anyway, Terrance I didn't call you to talk about my sad life story. Go on tell me all about what's been going on with you? Are you gonna call him?"

"I don't think so," I said.

"Why not?"

"Well to make a long story short. I don't know what I'm going to say...yet. Tori I just wanted to touch basis with you since we haven't talk to each other in a while, I have to get myself ready for work tomorrow."

"Ok," Tori retorted.

"I still work at the warehouse, but I have another job at the food court, too."

"Oh ok! The food court downtown?"

"Yes. That's the one."

"Well, maybe I'll stop by to see you sometime."

"That will be great. Tori, please call Carla. I think she needs someone to talk to. When I saw her, I couldn't talk to her like I wanted because I was working at the time. But give her a call from the both of us, ok?"

After I hung up, I looked in on my Mama. She was still sleep. The next morning, I whispered in her ear.

"I'm leaving for work and will see you later, Mama."

****

PATRICIA

Around 8:00 PM or so, I called Ray.

"I really miss you. Can you come over for dinner tonight?"

Ray arrived at about 9:00PM. I greeted him as always. I was all over him showing love and that I missed him. I really was happy to see him. I talked to Ray like I always did so that he wouldn't know that I knew all about him and his extracurricular activities. We had dinner, talked, and laughed like we always did before.

"Pat, what was your problem and reason for kicking me out?"

"Let's not talk about that right now. I was just out of my mind. I was really sick."

"What was wrong with you baby?"

"It doesn't really matter. What matters is that I'm good now, Ray."

"Anyway, how have you been? Are you OK?" I rubbed the side of his face gently with my hand.

"Hell, I feel good!" He smiled looking at me like a T-bone steak.

"I really miss you woman." It took every ounce of me to hold up my strength long enough to cook Ray's favorite dish, fried chicken with homemade macaroni and cheese.

"You look good enough to eat right now, Pat, and you still look fine as wine."

"Oh yeah, I'm glad you mentioned wine because I almost forgot it. Let me go get it." Ray smiled and nodded his head.

"That sounds good baby. Let's have that in the bedroom." I turned up my lip in a disgusting way.

"That would be great Ray!"

He went into the bedroom as I headed into the kitchen. I split open three capsules I was prescribed by the doctor to help me with falling asleep and when my pain was too unbearable. I shook the contents of the capsules into Ray's glass of wine. When I entered the bedroom, I gave Ray the glass as I sat back down on the bed. Ray grabbed me but I pulled away from him.

"Wait Ray let's talk for a little while."

"Talk about what woman? I miss your ass. You know I still love you, right?" He grabbed me again.

"Hold up Ray. Let me finish my wine," I romantically uttered.

"Hurry up baby because I'm gonna tear that ass up!" Ray gobbled down his wine as I eagerly watched him finish it all. I stalled for a while until I saw Ray yawn slowly leaning his head back against the headboard.

"Ray let's talk. I haven't seen you in weeks." Ray yawned

again confirming the drugs are going into full effect.

"Talk baby??" He looked at me sideways. "We got all night to fuck, talk, and sleep. Turn around girl and let me hit that big ass from behind before I go to sleep on your ass." His eyes started getting glassy.

"Humph, I bet you do want to hit it from behind," I said to Ray as he tried fumbling with his condom.

"Why you always grabbing a condom, Ray?"

"Come on baby. Let's reminisce later."

Slowly yet seductively, I hoisted my nightgown up and got on top of Ray.

"Ohhh, yes, that's what I'm talking about, baby."

"You like me in this position, huh?" Ray smiled hard.

"Yes and other ones too."

I leaned over and whispered into his ear. "Yeah, you love that face down ass up position too." Ray nodded anxiously.

"Yeah, Ray. I know! You like giving it in the ass or someone putting it in your ass, don't you?" Ray hesitated for a second.

"Woman, what are you talking about!?"

"You love me Ray, don't you?"

"Yeah I do, woman," Ray said.

"Then why the hell are you gay!?!"

"What you talkin' about woman!" My anger was boiling

over.

"RAYMOND! ARE YOU GAY?!" Ray was too tired to fight with me. Dryly he replied.

"HELL NO! What the hell are you talkin' about?" You could smell the lies coming from Ray let alone see it.

"You are such a liar! You're not even convincing. Why the hell! Do you always use condom, every time we make love. I just want you to know Ray that using those things on me didn't work mothafucka!" I knew the pills were working. Ray was stuck. He couldn't move.

I lost it. Not only was he trying to take me for everything I had. He broke me. I was still straddled on top of him. I leaned over and reached for the butcher knife I had underneath the pillow and plunged it deep into his chest. By this time, he tried to move but he couldn't. The pill had done just what I hoped it would do.

"You gay mothafucka!" I savagely tore the knife from out of his chest and drove it back in...again and again!

"You low down dirty dog. You knew you was fucking gay men, but you still pursued me. You knew you like men fucking you in the ass! Why did you come to me every night? You gave me motherfucking AIDS!! You gave me AIDS!"

Ray was frozen and didn't move. He tried to open his mouth but nothing would come out. One pill would put an elephant out. But I gave him three. I couldn't stop stabbing him.

"You took me away from my son! Now I'm going to die with this damn disease. My son won't have his mother anymore. And since I won't have my son, your lover's won't have you and I stabbed him right in the heart. Mama was so mad that she just continued to stab him over and over again. I finally stop stabbing him then looked down at his now limp dick.

"...and this dirty infected piece of shit!" I commenced to stabbing it over and over. I left his now partially severed dick hanging by just a vein.

When I came to reality, I was stunned by the savage stabbing I dealt him. I couldn't believe that I just killed my man. I shook my head then thought to myself...*Oh yeah, he wasn't mine's! Ray was everybody's man, men included.* I knew that I was going to prison for a long time for what I just did.

****

I finally got off of work. When I got home, I called out for my Mama but when she didn't answer I went to her room.

"What...the...fuck!?" I saw Ray lying in a puddle of blood on the bed. My heart started pounding through my chest. I couldn't breathe.

"Mama! Mama! Where are you! When he turned around she was balled up in the corner crying.

"I'm over here T. I.... I don't know what I've done."

"Mama did he hurt you? What happen here Mama? What happened?" I was confused. I never saw so much blood. It was everywhere.

"Mama, please tell me what happened. Did Ray hurt you?" I was whispering like someone could hear me

"I killed him! I killed that son of a bitch!"

"Mama! What happen! What's going on? We have to call the police and tell them that he assaulted you." I was now on my knees cradling over to my Mama, who was soaked in blood from head to toe.

"No! That's not what happened, T. I killed that nasty son of a bitch!" Mama was now staring over at the deceased body on the bed.

"Ok tell me why? What did he do?!"

"Baby," Mama paused. "This is gonna be the hardest thing that I have to tell you." She took a deep sigh as she began to cry.

"Mama, please stop crying. Tell me what happened here?

"Baby...baby, your Mama," she cleared her throat and paused.

"What Mama? Your mama is sick baby. I don't know how to tell you this, but I have to let you know..."

"Know what Mama? Just tell me Mama. What's wrong?"

"Your Mama has AIDS. I have full-blown AIDS,

Terrance...and I'm going to die." Ray gave this to me. He was living a double life and having sex with me and men. He infected me with this shit!" Mama then tapped my arm to help her up.

"I couldn't...I wouldn't let this man go around infecting other people with his lies or playing them the way he played me."

"I didn't...I didn't think about it. I just did it, T. I was so hurt, mad, angry, afraid, and full of rage. All I could think about is that I wasn't going to be around for you. He stole my future life from you without my permission." Mama continued crying.

"Mama listen, listen to me," I shouted out while shaking her.

"Are you listening Mama." Her head was now hanging low.

"Yes baby, I'm listening."

"Ok. We have to call the police. We have to get our story together, Mama.

"What are you talking about T? I killed him."

"Ok. ok. I get that Mama. But that's not the story we're going to tell the police, ok?"

"Baby what are you talking about?"

"Listen Mama, I can't lose you. I can't let you go to jail. Not now, not ever!" Tears began rolling down my face and I tried stopping them, but I failed...miserably.

"Mama you're sick and I can't let you go to jail. When the

cops come, please don't say anything." Mama looked at me sideways. I could tell she was oblivious as to what I was about to say.

"Mama, I did this, ok. Not you." Mama yelled.

"No! T. I won't let you do this, baby. I won't and that's that!"

"Mama please, please just listen to me for once!" I screamed out. "Let me take charge for once, Mama...for once!"

Finally, Mama began settling down allowing me to take lead. I wiped the tears from her face and escorted her to the living room, pointing for her to sit down on the couch.

"Where's the knife at that you used?"

She pointed to the bedroom and told me it's still on the bed next to Ray. After I retrieved the knife, I wiped off my Mama's fingerprints. I then proceeded to put Ray's blood on my clothes and my fingerprints all over the knife. I then had my Mama to change her clothes, put it in a bag, and hid them in the crawl space in my bedroom behind my dresser. I then instructed her to put on a skirt and blouse, and then I proceeded to plant Ray's blood on them.

"Mama, we got to rip your shirt to make it look like he was trying to rape you, ok?" She nodded quickly. We then went back into her bedroom to put Ray's pants back on to hide his partially severed penis because it was just hanging by a vein on the side of his balls. I then sat Mama down in the living room to call 911 but before she dialed the numbers, I signaled for her to hand me the phone.

"Give me the phone Mama. Let me do all the talking." As I was heading to the kitchen to make the call, Mama was once again having second and third thoughts.

"T, I...I can't let you do this, baby," she pleaded again.

"MAMA! Please, I got this. I won't be able to handle it if you go to prison so let me take care of this."

"Ok Mama! The police are on their way. Now let's go over our story again before the police get here." Mom and I went over what I was going to tell the police, making sure both our stories remain the same. I told her to please just follow along.

The police arrived. When they knocked on the door, I instantaneously transformed into acting mode. As I was opening the door, I almost forgot my script that I had been preparing myself for once I found myself starring down the barrel of a police issued Glock .10 mm. The police had guns pointing directly at me with clothes full of blood.

I quickly threw my hands up in the air pleading for them to not shoot and that my Mama was raped. One police officer went into police training mode.

"Turn around and put your hands behind your back!" I tried to tell them that I'm innocent but he became more aggressive. "Don't move I said!" The officer continued man handling me as I screamed out that I'm innocent but my pleas fell on deaf ears as he placed me in handcuffs. I couldn't believe what was happening.

"I'm innocent! My Mama was raped and I defended her!" Instead, my face was being mashed into the wall by now two officers.

My Mama was frantic. Her motherly instinct kicked in causing her to rush over to me but was stopped by another officer.

"That's my son! That's my son! He was protecting me!" She screamed out trying to wiggle free. The other police officers proceeded into the bedroom to access the crime scene. They found Ray lying in a puddle of blood on the bed.

"Ma'am, can you tell me what happened here?"

"He was trying to rape me!"

"When I came home, I heard my Mama screaming for him to get off of her. He had my Mama on the bed with her clothes ripped. She was screaming for him to get off of her. I then ran to the kitchen and snatched a knife from the wooden block and rushed back into the bedroom. I yelled for him to get off of her and that he was hurting my Mama."

I was running out of breath trying to explain everything to the officer. "I then grabbed him from off my Mama and we begin tussling. The next thing I knew, I was stabbing him over and over to protect my Mama. Everything then went black and I don't know what happened after that."

"Ma'am, is that what happened here?" Mama looked at the officer and nodded her head yes. An officer yelled from the bedroom that the suspect is deceased and to call the medical examiner. We have a homicide.

The officer looked from my Mama to me.

"We're going to need a written statement from you."

I looked at my Mama with much concern, hoping that she gets the story right. Before she was escorted away from the scene, I heard my Mama tell them everything just like I told her to say.

The detectives arrived and began taking pictures of the crime scene. Mama was told that she couldn't stay in the house until after she gets clearance to return.

After I was read my Miranda rights, I was immediately removed from our house and placed in the back of the police car. I was in tears watching as they finished wrapping the yellow crime scene tape around the exterior of the house.

"What are you doing to my son?"

"Ma'am, he's under arrest for murder. We're taking him to jail to be processed for murder. An ambulance is on the way to take you to the hospital to get examined and we'll have someone to meet you there to take your statement.

"I don't need an ambulance! I need to know where are you taking my son and when can I see him?"

"After he has been arraigned, ma'am."

The coroner came in to take the body to the morgue. An officer came over to Mama and told her again that she could not stay here tonight. Mama did not know where she was going. She only had one good friend and that was her friend Delores. She called Delores crying hysterically asking her if she can come get her because something bad just happened here. Delores said without hesitation *I'm on my way*!

The officer was nice to let Mama wait for her ride. When Delores came the officer would not let her into the apartment instead he told her that this is an active crime scene.

"I'm here to pick up my friend," D said. The officer told me my ride was here. I came out with my bag in my hand, still crying but not before I shoved the bag that I hid in the back of T's closet in my suitcase with Ray blood on it. I couldn't leave it behind. The police then took my baby to jail.

"What happened here Pat?" Delores asked.

"Just get me out of here!" I shouted.

As me and Delores got into the car, she turned to me.

"Patricia, I love you and the whole nine yards but I am not moving this vehicle from here until you tell me what is going on.

"Drive! Just drive!" I screamed out. As Delores was driving away, I broke down.

"D, Terrance killed Ray!"

"What!" She then paused. "Why!? What happened?"

"I knew I had to stick to the story Terrance and I agreed to stick with. As much as I wanted to tell her everything, I couldn't tell her the truth. I did not want to mess nothing up and end up in jail especially with my critical condition.

"D, Ray was trying to hurt me. My baby jumped in an stab him."

"WHAT!! Stabbed him where?"

"In his heart." I didn't want to mention the slicing of his penis. Delores is my very best friend. She has three children, who are all grown and living their best lives with their own families. Delores lived by herself and had her significant friends over from time to time. She was one who loved her space and only shared it when she wanted to.

Once we arrived and I got settled down, I wanted to tell my best friend everything that's going on with my health.

"There's something I really need to talk to you about and I don't know where to start."

"First Pat, let me ask, are you ok? You just don't look too well. Did Ray hurt you?"

I took a deep sigh. "Yes he really did", I said.

"You said you've been out of work for over a month or so now. Why? What's going on with you my friend?"

I hesitated because I didn't know where to begin, or how D would react so I just spilled everything out.

"I have full blown AIDS, Delores." I was now balled up on the couch crying hysterically.

D seemed like she didn't hear the word AIDS. Instead, she just turned around and heads to her linen closet to get me a blanket. When she returned, I was now laid out on the sofa pretending to be asleep. I wasn't ready to tell D the real truth but I wanted too! Just not tonight.

All I could think about was Terrance and how he was doing. I couldn't understand why he would take the fault for me. She couldn't wrap her head around what just happen and why Ray did this to her and how long have he been playing the faker game about him being gay. My mind was all over the place with why questions. I couldn't wait until the morning came so I could go to the jail to see what was going on with my son.

When morning came D left for work without waking me Up. When I woke up it, was 12 o'clock in the afternoon.

"OMG! As I got up to get myself together, my body, mind, and soul was moving slow because I wasn't feeling well.

I arrived at the jail around 1:15 in the afternoon. The officer that took my information told me that Terrance's arraignment was at 9:00 this morning and he was not given a bond. He will have to stay in jail until his court date. The officer advised me that I need to get a lawyer because my son is looking at a lot of time for murder.

The detective that was at the house saw me and asked if I could come into his office. My tears wouldn't stop falling. What am I going to do without my baby? And what did the detective want to talk to me about? As I was entering his office, he motioned for me to sit in the chair diagonal from his desk. He didn't waste any time asking me questions.

"I'm going to just get straight to the point ma'am. Are you sure that you and your son are telling us the whole story of what happened with Mr. Holden?"

"Yes, why?"

"Ok so can you tell me how Mr. Holden penis got practically severed?"

"I don't know. I guess my son did it during their struggle." I wanted to say, *that nigga gave me AIDS with that infected thing and I tried to cut it off.* But I remembered that Terrance told me to stick to the story. I had so many thoughts going on in my mind. I wanted to tell the police that I killed Ray and why, but Terrance's voice kept shouting around in my head telling me to be quite because he got this.

Finally, I left the jail and the detective's office. I was

crying as I was walking to the bus stop. I knew that I was going to have to tell D the whole story. I felt so bad having to call on my best friend to help me. I haven't been a good friend to her lately ever since Ray came into my life.

When I met Ray, my friendship with D stopped and our phone calls went from every day to every once in a while. The only time we did speak to one another was when D would call me. After arriving home, D came in the house. I was sitting there with my hands on my head thinking about what I was going to say to her, as well as what I was going to do about my son situation.

"Pat, we need to figure out what you going to do about everything that has happened. First I need to know what's going on." I could see the deep concern written all over D's face.

I looked at her as she sat down next to me.

"Honey, I want to know other than what just happen with Ray, if you are ok?" I looked up at D puzzled as they both sat next to one another on the sofa.

"What do you mean?"

"Pat, we've been friends for years and although we might not have been around each other like we use to, I still know when something doesn't look right with you. We both fell quiet before D continued.

"What's going on with you friend?" Then out of nowhere, my tears were flowing like a Tsunami and they wouldn't stop.

"I can't tell you because I feel dirty and I don't want to be judged by my only friend right now and with T in jail I don't have anyone. I don't know what to do!"

"Shhhhh, I'm here friend. Honey you have me. What's going on? Why did T kill Ray? He was the love of your life. You stop dealing with everybody for that man. You really shut everyone down for him. What happen?"

"I know and I'm so sorry D. I thought he was the one and I was going to spend the rest of my life with that man. I guess the joke was on me."

"What do you mean Pat?" I looked up at D and cried even harder.

"What's wrong honey?"

"D, I am dying." The room fell eerily quiet.

"Wait. What!?" Patricia, what are you saying? What are you saying?"

"I don't know where to start. T told me not to say anything that he was going to take care of it."

"How Pat? How is he going to take care of something like this? How?"

"D, I've been very sick lately. My baby has been holding us down with a job because I have nearly used up all of my savings."

"How come Pat. Talk to me honey. What's going on with

you, friend?"

"There is too much going on in my life right now and I don't need anyone to judge me or have sympathy for me either."

"Well for Christ's sake, just tell me. Tell me what's going on? We've been too close of friends for too many years, whether or not we see or talk to each other every day. You will always be my best friend. I will never judge you. Please talk to me, please."

Delores could feel the tension.

"D, I'm sick."

"Ummm, ok and I know you're not feeling well. You'll get better friend."

"No D you don't know!"

"Know what Pat?"

"D...I...I..." I paused trying not to cry again.

"Pat, maybe I can help you. Whatever it is, we will get through it together.

"Not with *this* friend. Not with this." I wiped away a tear that snuck down my cheek.

"What is it? Tell me why you keep crying?

"D, I don't know how to tell you something like this. Or even where to begin. Just talk to me Patricia. You can tell me anything." I paused for the last time before telling her the story.

"D, I'm not just sick I'm dying."

"What! OMG! You have cancer or something?"

"I have the 'or something. I have full blown AIDS, D."

D looked at me with fear in her eyes, trying to collect what she just heard me tell her.

"What are you talking about Patricia? What do you mean you have full blown AIDS? What are you talking about!?" D was frozen. I guess what I'd just revealed to her hadn't hit her yet.

"D, I haven't been a good friend to you. When I met Ray I forgot about our friendship and fell head over hills with his words. I thought I had it all together. I was blinded by love and I lost the true meaning of a friend who really loved me." I took a deep breath before continuing.

"D, Ray wasn't who I thought he was."

"Pat, what are you saying to me right now? That! I'm going to lose my best friend?" I started crying more.

"Yes, D! That dirty nigga was gay and gave me AIDS!"

"What! So, help me make sense of this Pat. What exactly are you saying?" D couldn't believe what she was hearing from me. She knew there was something weird about Ray. She just couldn't tell me because I was so gone over him.

"Ok, ok Pat. But you can still live a long life with AIDS."

"Not this time D. The doctor said that I have full blown AIDS and it's attacking my cells and rapidly. It's just a matter of months before I die."

D hugged me as if I was taking my last breath now.

"Everything will be alright," D said trying to be convincing.

"Yes D, but what am I supposed to do about my baby? He's in jail. How am I supposed to help him if I'm dying?"

"Does T know this Pat?"

"Yes. That's why he said that he will take care of the murder situation."

"How Patricia? How? They have him for murder!"

"I know. I don't know what to do. I need to talk to T." I placed both my hands on top of my head.

"Lordy, what am I supposed to do? T Took care of me and all the bills. T stepped up to the plate and held things down for his mama. Now I have to help my son. He doesn't belong in a place like that." D walked over to the dining room table but we could still see and hear one another.

"What happened when you went to the court today?"

"I was late, so I won't know what's going on until he calls me and tell me what happened. All I know is that he was given a court appointed attorney."

"Pat, we have to get him a lawyer." I agreed.

"I know D, but who??

"I know of someone who can represent him. Do you want me to give him a call?"

"Yes, but I don't know how I'm going to pay them. I don't

have any money."

"Let's just talk to him."

The next morning while I was still asleep, D went to go see her lawyer friend. She knew that I was exhausted. When I woke up, D was coming into the house.

"I didn't want to wake you but I went to talk to my lawyer friend. He agreed that he would look into the case and he'll get back to me. I'll let you know what my next move will be. I told him as much as I possibly knew including your terminal illness and how you contracted the AIDS Virus from the man that Terrance 'allegedly' killed."

"What do you mean *allegedly*?" The lawyer stated that because until he has all the facts pertaining to the case, no one can be accused until found guilty by a court of law." D continued,

"He's going to look into Terrance case and get back to us to let us know what is going on."

I just looked at D.

"I wanted to go with you. I didn't want to put all of my problems on you. I didn't contact you so that you can help me get out of this situation." D look at me.

"I understand that Pat but we are friends till the end and I will not leave you alone if there is something that I can do, I will do all that I can."

D noticed I wasn't feeling too well.

"You don't look too good baby. Maybe you should lay down a little bit more." I glanced over at D.

"I will not rest or sleep until I'm in the grave and know that my baby boy is alright."

Weeks went by before D and I heard from the lawyer. He advised us that he would take on T's case. And what made this even a blessing, he said that he would do it as a pro bono case. But for the life of me, everything about this story doesn't make any sense. I can't understand why they locked him up especially with it being self-defense.

"Pat, Mr. Miller called to say that he would like to set up a meeting with you so you two can go over Terrance's case. We agreed to meet next Thursday. Terrance is scheduled for a bond hearing Monday. When Mr. Miller and I met, instead of it being at his office, it was at D's house because I was too ill to travel.

Once Mr. Miller arrived, he came in the house and went straight to the case at hand.

"Hello Ms. Patricia," he said with his hand extended out to shake mine.

"I'm just gonna get straight to the point ma'am. Is there anything about this story that you and you son might've left out because I can only help you two if I know the whole story." I shot him a look as to say, *what the hell do you mean the whole story*.

"I told you everything I know, Mr. Miller." I hesitated

because I knew what I had promised T.

I was so sick the entire weekend. I was vomiting and urinating and having bowel movements on myself. Thank God for my friend Delores because I was almost bed ridden.

"Pat, I really need you to let me take you to the doctor because your health is deteriorating.

"No D! I have to try to get myself better so I can be at my son's court date on Monday."

"If you are unable to make it, I will go in your place baby, ok?"

"I know D. You are such a loyal and trusted friend. Not only that, you are so good to me...but I have to talk to my son. I just have to."

I knew my days were marked and that I wouldn't be around to carry on this lie much longer. I also knew that I couldn't let my baby sit in jail for a crime that I committed. At this point in my life, I have nothing to lose except my future with my baby.

I called out to D, who was in the kitchen fixing me some chicken broth. When she came over to me, I shot her a frightening look.

"What's wrong friend?" D was obviously worried about my health withering away.

"D, I have something to tell you except I just can't right this moment. But trust me that I will in due time." D looked at me and wondered what could it be.

"D, I need to know that you will be there for T. when I'm gone."

"Friend, you're going to be alright baby." I immediately became enraged because she doesn't want to face the reality that I'm dying.

"No D! I'm really dying and it's just a matter of time! Please promise me that you will be there for my son! Please!" D knew by the tone in my voice I was serious.

"I will Pat and you know that." I let out a sigh of relief and unknowingly passed out on the couch.

Monday finally arrived. Me and D went to the court hearing together. We spotted Mr. Miller first.

"How are you feeling Ms. Patricia?" I felt at ease knowing he was very concerned regarding my declining health.

"Can I talk to my son before they call his case?"

"No ma'am. That's not likely especially with the severity of the charges that's he's facing but I'll see if you would be able to see him being that he is still legally a minor but being charged as an adult. But let's see after the judge finish seeing him." I nodded.

Terrance's name was finally called. His bond was denied again and was being sent back to the jail until the next court hearing. My heart took a deep dive into sorrow. Upon further investigation of this case, I learned that the prosecutor hasn't gathered up enough evidence. Mr. Miller told me that it looks good for T because they are still trying to put together evidence to charge him with. I looked at Mr. Miller and pleaded with him to let me see my son.

"Give me a moment, Ms. Patricia. I'll see what I can do."

They agreed to allow me to go in the back area where he was being detained so that I could see T. I had to see and talk to him through the plexiglass window that had a phone attached to it. I was so happy to see my baby.

T looked at me with a big smile on his face. Not to mention mine was just as big. After T did a look over my frail body, his smile soon turned upside down.

"Mama, I'm so glad to see you. Mama you don't look too good. Are you taking your med'?"

"Yes baby I am. But we can talk about that later because they didn't give us a lot of time so please listen honey." Terrace face was now showing fear.

"Mama is really sick and I can't or I don't think I'm going to make it too much longer especially with you in here. Baby they won't lock me up because I'm dying."

"Mama stop. Please stop. I got this. Just remember what you promised."

"Well, baby I just want you to promise me that you would reach out to your dad and my family if anything happens to me, ok T?"

He looked at me as I looked back at him.

"T, please promise me that." The officers came over to advise our time was up. I kissed the glass with tears in my eyes and told T that he will be out soon.

"T, I will always love you and be with you always!" I shouted at the glass window.

T. looked at me as if it would be the last time he would see me and then started to cry.

When D and I got home, I was so exhausted. No sooner than I laid down on the couch, I fell asleep. Later on, that morning while still lying down, I began choking. I tried to catch my breath but failed and crashed to the floor. D ran in and immediately called the ambulance who came and rushed me to the hospital.

Once I arrived at the hospital, they immediately hooked me up to a lot of machines. After my blood work came back, I was told that I need to call my family because my T-Cell count was at a dangerous level. They don't know how long I have. I asked for my friend D and told her that it didn't look to good and that I was dying. D began to cry and I told her to stop and that I really needed to tell her something.

I told D everything including how I was the actual one that killed Ray because he gave me full blown AIDS and how T made her promise not to tell no one that she did it. The room fell silent. You could hear a pin drop.

"Pat, what? What?!" I nodded my head yes.

"D, listen. I need you to do something for my son please. Can you go back to your house, look in the bottom of my luggage that I put in the back of your closet. You will find my gown with Ray's blood on it. Please bring it to me. I have a letter I need you to sign." I began moaning from the excruciating pain I was in. No pain medicines could kill it. My life was now on borrowed time.

"He didn't do this Delores. It was me! The letter has my confession on it. I stated that I was the one who committed the crime. I, alone, killed Ray and the reason being is because I was devastated when I found out that he had affected me with this virus. It states in my letter that my son was not home at the time. I needed D to be my witness to me signing this confession, but before I sign it, I requested to see the detective that gave me his business card as well as Mr. Miller. I also went on to express to D what she promised me.

"You remember what you promise me, right? You promised that you will take care of my son."

"Pat, that's without question. I got you and T."

"D, there's something else that I need you to do for me."

"Anything. I got you friend." I then grabbed a hold of D's shaking hand.

"Make sure T go and see my mother and his dad. I just

want him to know that he has a family, please D."

"I will ok." Delores then placed a phone call to both Mr. Miller and the detective to inform them of all that's going on with me now being on my death bed. D strongly advised them that I needs to see them ASAP she told them both that she didn't think that I was going to make it through the remainder of the day.

After a couple of hours passed, I was awoken by someone knocking on my room door. Mr. Miller came in and as soon as he got there, the detective arrived as well.

I began wincing in pain then started choking on my saliva Mr. Miller looked at me and asked how long have I been like this.

"She's been sick for a long time now. Mr. Miller and Detective Alston, Patricia has something she want you both to know."

I showed them my confession.

"I needed to sign this in front of witnesses because I'm dying and I don't want my son to take on my demons. I beg you to please help my son. I'm dying and I don't know if I can hold on any longer. Please get my son out of that jail. He's innocent. I killed Ray."

They both read my confession and ask me is this a true statement. As I was nodding yes, I handed them the nightgown that I had Delores retrieve from my suitcase that was in her closet.

"Please test it for DNA. My son was not there. He arrived after I killed him and he didn't want to see me die in jail from being ill. So he said he did it, but he didn't. He's going to be upset that I'm breaking my promise to him which was to let him take the fall. Please let him know that I did this for him and I couldn't die knowing that he was in prison for a crime that I committed."

The detective looked at Mr. Miller and vowed that they would do everything they had to do to get him out. They will try to get him here before I take my last breath. The doctors told them that it was going to be soon.

"Ms. Freeman," the detective began. "I need you to know that Mr. Holden didn't test positive for AIDS."

"WHAT! What do you mean?" I began to cry immediately.

"Ma'am you didn't contract this virus from him. Can you think of anyone else you might have contracted this virus from?" Once Detective Alston stated that to me, I screamed out.

"No! Noooo! Terrance!" I went into cardiac arrest.

DELORES

The doctors tried to revive her but she was gone. Everyone looked at each other in shock. I looked at Mr. Miller, with tears rolling down my face.

"What are we going to do now?" I asked looking from Detective Alston to Mr. Miller. The detective shrugged his shoulders.

"Why? Would you tell her that you'll take care of everything! You need to get Terrance out of there." I shouted out to the detective. Then Mr. Miller agreed causing Detective Alston to simultaneously agree.

"I will make the necessary arrangements to have him release soon as possible." Mr. Alston said.

When I got home I sat on the couch crying and thinking about my promise that I made to my friend. There is no doubt in her mind that I wasn't going to be there for my friend and godson. I got myself together and started preparing the spare room that Pat was in. I prayed that I could be strong for him as well as myself, because even though I haven't had much time with my friend, due to going our separate ways. I never gave up on our friendship. I just never knew at what cost she would return.

It took about two days before hearing from Mr. Miller who stated that T was being released and that nobody told him yet about his mother passing. I knew that I had to be strong for Terrance. I knew that this would be hard for him to take.

Once Terrance came through the gates, he was looking around for his mother.

"Aunt D, where's my Mama. I told her that I got this." T chuckled because that's her favorite saying. "*She got this.*"

"I'm sorry Aunt D. I'm glad you're here, but where's Mama? Is she still feeling under the weather today?" It pained me to put on a temporary fake smile while telling him to just get into the car and we can talk more about your mother.

When they got into the car, I just didn't know how to break the bad news to him about the death of his mother."

"Terrance, I don't know how to say this to you, in a way that it won't hurt."

"What Aunt D! What do you have to say?"

"Umm, well Terrance...your mother confessed on Monday that she killed Ray."

"What! I told her not to say anything and that I would take care of it."

"Baby, she knew you would but she had to get her baby out of there. It was making her even sicker knowing that you were behind bars for something that she had done."

"That's not what I wanted for her. I just wanted her to relax and let me go through it. I didn't want her to go through this shit in her condition. What did they do to her? Where is she?"

"She knew that Terrance, but she couldn't hold it together knowing that you were in there because of her."

"What Aunt D? What are you saying?!" Terrance was angry and rightfully so.

"Take me home Aunt D. Take me to my Mama. I need to talk to her!" I paused for a moment before telling my godson the hardest thing I've ever had to tell someone.

"Terrance, baby I'm so sorry, but...your mother is gone. She died Monday evening." We were both still sitting in my car. We hadn't even left the parking lot of the jail.

"What! No! No! No! My Mama ain't dead!" He shouted.

"She's gone baby."

"Stop Aunt D! Please take me to my mother, now!"

"Terrance, I'm so sorry baby but Pat's went on home."

"NOOOO! Stop! She wouldn't leave me. She knew I needed her."

"Baby, she left you in my care and you can stay with me as long as you want. I'm your Godmother and I'm here to step in to do my part."

Terrance continued bawling like a baby. I comforted him as best as I knew how. He finally stopped crying to ask me where his Mama was?

"She's at the funeral home now. They are waiting to see

what we're going to do."

"Aunt D, I don't know the first thing about funerals or what to do."

"Well baby that's what I'm here for...to help you. Your mother wanted me to tell you one more thing."

"What?" He was curious yet anxious.

"She wanted me to give you the address where your grandparents are so you could reach out to them." Terrance's face was full of anger.

"What!? No! Why would she want me to do that? I don't want to know anything about that man or my grandparents. They brought too much pain in Mama's life and I think it hurt her so bad that she could never get herself together after that."

"Well Terrance, this was your mother's last wish on her dying bed and I had to tell you what she wanted me to let you know. Also, Terrance there is one more thing that I have to let you know..." Just when he thought he couldn't take no more bad news, I had to add more injury to his pain.

"What Aunt D! What else can it be?"

"Your mother learned just before she died that she didn't contract the AIDS virus from Ray. He was found negative of the virus."

"Wait...What! No! I don't believe that."

"Baby, that's what the detective told your momma before

she passed away. I think once she found out, she went into a deep place and she couldn't handle it. Her last word was '*No!*' Terrance. Do you know what she was trying to say?"

"No? I don't know! I don't know!" he screamed out. The rest of the drive to the funeral home was in complete silence. We arrived at the funeral home so Terrance could see his mother. Terrance stared at her for a long time lying in the coffin. She looked so peaceful. A smile appeared upon his face. He knew his mother was no longer in pain suffering anymore. Even though he is going to miss his mother he knew that she was in a better place.

TERRANCE

Although, I was hurting I felt the peace for my Mama. I sat in the funeral parlor for what seem like hours. Aunt D gave me my space. Once I was finished spending time with Mama, I went back to Aunt D's place. I told her that I was going to seek out my family to see if they would like to come to my Mama's home going.

I couldn't believe that my family only lived two hours away from us and they never try to come see me. We took the ride from Philadelphia to Maryland to see them. When I got to my grandmother's house, she opened the door and didn't even know who I was.

"Hi grandma." She became quiet and still as she was surveying all of me from my head to my toes.

"Oh my goodness! Your mother let you come see us?"

I was thrown back because she didn't even say-'hello, how are you. I'm glad to meet you. Nothing. It was at that very moment I fully understood my Mama's reasons for keeping me away. The coldness was felt by both me and Aunt D.

"No, she didn't."

"Ok so where is my daughter? She never sent a card to tell us what she had or what your name was...nothing!" Damn, she still hadn't invited us in. Wow.

"My name is Terrance Oliver Mitchell, Jr."

"What!" she replied as if I said something wrong!

"*She* named you Terrance?"

"Yes *she* did," I shot back but not meaning to be disrespectful. As my new grandmama went to hug me, I back up.

"I'm sorry but I don't know you."

"I'm sorry baby. I'm your grandmother, Ms. Claudia. You two can come on in. Don't mind my ill manners. I apologize," she looked both me and Aunt D up and down, then motioned with her hand for us to have a seat in her living room.

"So, how's your mother doing and where is she?"

I sat there temporarily numb to the question.

"I'm here only because meeting you was my Mama's last wish."

"What do you mean her last wish?"

"My Mama gone. She died!" I said with so much built up anger. My grandmama looked at me and Aunt D and she collapsed in her chair.

"Oh my god! Oh my god! What...What happened to my daughter?" I ignored her question and asked her one of my own.

"Do you know where my sperm donor is at?" She gazed at me then suddenly her face had misery cast all over it.

"Terrance, I'm so sorry but your dad also died."

"What you mean my dad is also dead? When did this happened? How...why? Why didn't somebody at least try to reach out to us."

"I didn't think your mother cared to know anything about him."

"But he was my father, right!?"

"Yes, baby he was."

"Well didn't anybody think that I've should have at least been given the chance to make that decision on my own. When did this happen? How did he die?"

"Well baby your dad..." she paused. "He died two years ago. Your dad died from AIDS, baby."

"No! No!" I jumped up.

"What are you saying to me! What are you saying to me?"

I felt like a ton of bricks landed on my chest.

"You mean to tell me that bastard gave that shit to my Mama?" My grandmama looked at me with tears in the webs of her eyes.

"Terrance, baby what are you saying?"

"My Mama died from full blown AIDS. She thought that her man gave it to her, so she killed him! She murdered a man because she found out that he was gay and she thought he gave her the AIDS virus. All the while she contracted it from my dad?"

"Well baby I think so because your Aunt Pam has the HIV as well." I was now standing up with my hands crossed on top of my head with my fingers locked together. I couldn't believe what I was hearing. This had to be a nightmare!

"Are you serious! Are you serious! She's dead too!?" Aunt D couldn't believe all of what we just learned. She was glued to the chair and couldn't move.

"No baby but she contracted the virus from your dad. She found out that he had AIDS when she got sick and they told her she tested positive for HIV. She knew that she contracted it from him, so he got tested and found out that he had the AIDS Virus. She had it for some years now."

"I'm so confused! So, you mean to tell me that you all knew this and you knew where we were at and you never bothered to let your daughter know?" I didn't even want to look my grandmama in the face. I was scared of what my anger might make me say or even do at this point. I then turned to face her because she needed to see the strength and love that she stole from me written all over my face.

"What did my Mama ever do to you for you to hate us so much, huh?"

"Terrance, your Mama was a good daughter. It was me. I was a lousy mother and I took sides over my children. I didn't know how to tell that to her. I never thought he gave it to her. I thought, she was the lucky one. I thought that she was the one that got away from that infected man. If I knew that he wasn't no good for my daughters, I would have never betrayed my daughter for that man. I would have sent him packing. Especially when he played my daughters against each other and broke their sisterly bond." I couldn't believe what I was hearing. Now she's trying to play victim.

"I never knew that he infected your mother too. I thought that she dodge that bullet. When I found out that your Aunt Pam contracted HIV from him, it hurt me to my heart. I wanted to kill him as well until she told me he had full blown AIDS and was dying. So, I figured Karma beat me to the punch."

"I thought Aunt Pam was pregnant around the same time My Mama was?"

"She was. She had a beautiful daughter name Amanda. Amanda was found to be virus free. Thank God. So, I assume you are too?"

Aunt D. Step in and answer that question before I could.

"Yes he is," she interjected even though she didn't know the answer to that question. At that time, Amanda had come in from another part of the house.

"Grandma, mommy wants to know if you were still taking her to the grocery store." We both looked at each other. Two strangers.

"Yes baby. I want you to meet your brother." Amanda looked at me puzzled.

"My brother? What's going on grandma?"

I looked at Amanda and knew that she was as clueless as I was. Nobody never told her the history about us being siblings and having the same father.

"Well, it seems that we are brother and sister *and* cousins all in one because our Mamas were fucking the same man. Wait, let me correct myself. He left my Mama for your Mama. Welp, least you got to know our father because he sure as hell didn't care to know anything about me."

"But we don't have anything to do with what those grownups did," said Amanda before continuing. "It seems to me like we were both just collateral damage. I do see our resemblance not to mention we look about the same age."

For some strange reason, it felt as if the thick tension in the air started dissipating.

"I'm sixteen Amanda and you?"

"I'm fifteen," Amanda said. I was still angry over all of this shocking news. I tried to remain calm but my emotions started getting the best of me.

"Well, my Mama had him first and then he started cheating around with your Mama. We are sister and brother, *and* cousin or whatever the hell we are."

"My Mama told me everything. Grandma took your Mama's side over mine's and that hurt my Mama to the core. What hurt her the most was when she found out that your Mama, her only sister was pregnant as well as her. My so-called dad decided to marry your Mama instead. That crush my Mama mentally, physically, and spiritually. She was broken and never bounced back. She couldn't live in the same town with them anymore. So, she moved and I never got to know him. My Mama was my best friend and my first love. I will miss her dearly." As much as I wanted to hate this girl sitting in front of me, my spirit wouldn't let me.

Amanda jumped up and said I'm so sorry to hear that. Please don't think that my mom had it so great. Her life was full of ups and downs with my dad." My grandmama looked at her perplexed.

"Amanda, honey, what are you saying?"

"Grandma, momma never wanted you to know what was going on behind our closed doors, but my daddy was no saint. Momma would put on a fake smile for you all the time." No sooner than she made that statement, the door opened and in pops Aunt Pam.

"Ma, what's taking you two so..." Aunt Pam stopped dead in her tracks when she saw us in the kitchen.

She looked from my grandmama to me to Aunt D, then over to her daughter.

"Hello, what's going on in here? What's wrong, Ma? Why are you so upset?"

"Pam, this is Patricia's son...your nephew."

"Wait...What?" Pam said with her face full of shock.

"Well, well, well. Hello nephew. I finally get the chance to see and meet you. Your very handsome."

"Hmmph, like my dad," I said sarcastically. She acted as if she didn't hear what I just said and then proceeded with her inquisitiveness.

"Sooo, how's my sister doing?" She said with a sly smirk on her face.

"Pam, Terrance came to tell us that your sister died."

"Died? What do you mean died? What happened and when? "She asked me.

"On Monday, a couple of days ago from AIDS that your husband gave her."

"Terrance, I know you hurting but please have respect for your Aunt." I looked at my grandmama and was getting ready to say something when Aunt D grab my hand.

"Well, we just came to tell you about her home going and..." I interrupted Aunt D.

"I thought I was going to meet my dad for the first time, but I guess I'm not missing nothing after all." I gave them the information on where and when the funeral was going to be held and told them they can attend if they like. The funeral was being held next Saturday and the viewing was Friday.

Monday, Aunt D took me to get tested just to make sure I didn't have HIV or AIDS. I was surprised we got my test results back Thursday the day before the viewing and learned I was indeed negative and in the clear for all municipal diseases. The day of the viewing, many people came out to show their respect for Mama, even some of Ray's friends. Grandma Claudia, Grandpa, Aunt Pam, and Amanda showed up. I was happy and sad at the same time. Feeling like it shouldn't have taken my Mama's death to bring us together.

I was so overwhelmed that everything turned out great thanks to Aunt D. She showed out and put her friend away well. Mama told Aunt D about a lot of things she didn't tell me. Which made this funeral go so well. The funeral was beautiful. The preacher did a wonderful job. I was so happy to see my friends Tori and Carla. I greeted the girls and thanked them for coming.

Carla looked at me and smiled.

"Remember Terrance, no matter what we will always be the CTT gang." I smiled for the first time in a long time. After the funeral, we went to the burial ground and that's when it hit me.

The reality of knowing I wasn't going to see Mama again ripped at me even more. Aunt D was still feeling some type of way because she didn't know if I was going to stay with her in Philadelphia or move with my newly found family and finish school in Maryland. Aunt D knew that Mama gave her custody of me, but she wanted me to make the decision on my life.

The conversation came up at the house when I told my grandparents that my Mama gave Aunt D, her best friend, custody of me. I'm staying with who I know. I agreed to stay in touch and build a bond with my sister.

The 11th grade went by so fast. Tori, Carla, and me were so busy with our own things that we barely got a chance to see each other. Then next thing you know, 12th grade would be the year for us to decide if they were going to make it, fake it, or fail.

I pursued my goal of going to school for dental hygienist. It's my hope to explore Temple University to learn all I need in becoming what I've been wanting since I could remember. I'm going to make my Mama proud. This was all we use to talk about. The 12th grade prom came and I took both Tori and Carla as my prom dates. We looked sharper than a kitchen knife in our outfits. We were colored coordinated and everyone loved it. We spent all evening enjoying ourselves at the prom together because we knew we were getting ready to go on our separate journeys.

Carla

~BREAKER~

Carla sat on the stoop at her house having flashbacks about her childhood. It felt like a twelve-ring boxing match as she fought with the horrible thoughts that were going on in her head. One minute she was happy and excited than in the next moment, she was sad and depressed. She didn't know what emotions she should stay with. So, she just laughed and cried simultaneously wondering what her life was going to be like now.

Carla is 14 years old and her brother Calvin is 16. Their Aunt Mimi received custody of both Carla and Calvin at a time in their lives where things were very awkward for them both especially with their Aunt Mimi having a set of five-year-old twin girls.

My brother and I had such a good life, at least I thought so. My mom and dad were the ideal couple...at least in my eyes. I loved the relationship they had. We did so many things as a family not to mention we went on many trips together. Our mom had her own hair salon and dad was the head man at the liquor store. Things were looking good for us all. Then Mama started getting tired all the time and daddy would ask her was everything ok. She would hang her head down low and say, *yeah.* Our daddy would give her a look of concern.

As time and years went by, we didn't get to go places any

more. She was tired all the time now and hardly went to the Salon or even cared to do my hair anymore.

One day dad came home feeling kind of tipsy. He told momma it was time to talk to the kids. I was wondering about what and why! Did momma even had the strength, energy, or the ability to even sit up to talk to us at all. She spent most of her days in bed.

This was around the time when Calvin was 12 and I was 10 years old. We all piled up in momma and daddy's room. Dad was sitting on the bed next to her crying like a baby.

"Ma, what's wrong?" Momma begin to tell us that she had cancer and was not going to be around much longer. She wanted us all to promise her that we would take care of each other. We all sat silent in the room for what seemed like forever until she had told us to go get something to eat.

Momma passed away in June and Daddy was a mess, to say the least. Everybody told Daddy that they would come and give him a hand with us kids, but once momma was gone, that never happened! We never got to see our grandmother or knew who she was until the day of the funeral. Momma never wanted to talk about her. Hell, she never let us even go over to our grandmother's house. She only told us that she was not a nice lady and she don't want to hear us mention the name *grandma* in our house. And we didn't. We always seen Aunt Mimi because she was always under momma. She was our mother's younger and only sibling. She always helped momma out in her hair salon or with us.

One day I heard my momma and Aunt Mimi talking. Aunt Mimi was crying about how she couldn't do it anymore and that she needed to come live with her. When I came into the room, they stopped talking and mama told me to go get the towels from out of the clothes dryer. I knew that was to just get me out the room. I could never figure out the sadness in Aunt Mimi's eyes.

Aunt Mimi stayed with us more than she stayed at home and grandma didn't seem to care. The last time we saw Aunt Mimi was the day of momma's funeral. She was yelling at my grandma about her never caring about her. Grandma pulled her arm back and slapped Aunt Mimi in the face causing her to run outside crying. Calvin and I didn't understand what was going on with grandma's kids or why they didn't want to be around her. Grandma never came to see any of us let alone give us any comfort or even a mere hug. It was ironic because in all those years we haven't seen her in our lives and just like that...she came into our lives and just like that, she left like a thief in the night.

Calvin and I started seeing our daddy most of the time, yet when we did he was drunk, high, or bringing different types of women in our mother's house. Daddy changed once she died. He was lost and just couldn't seem to get it together. It seemed like momma was the one who held daddy up. He started drinking more and more.

One night I heard him in the living room talking so I got up only to find out that there was nobody there. He was talking to momma like she was right in the room with him. Daddy lost his job at the liquor store and lost momma's salon too for not paying the bills and taxes. He stayed drunk and high all the time and he didn't even fight to keep what momma worked so hard to get. He had to find another job to keep us afloat. Calvin hung out in the streets most nights and I always found myself alone. Things got so bad at home that people started to talk about how our daddy was doing a poor job of taking care of us.

When Calvin and I came home one day there were two people waiting on the stoop for us.

"Carla and Calvin Jones?" the lady said. Calvin put his hand in front of me to stop me from responding back.

"...and who wants to know?" He said as a protective older brother would do. The lady told us she was from the children's services and needed to talk to us.

"About what? My father is not here right now," Calvin shot back with a bad attitude in full motion.

"Oh, we know. That's why we are here. My name is Mrs.

Long and this is Mr. Bartell," she goes pointing to her partner.

"Like I explained before, we're from the Children's Services and we need to go inside and have a talk with you two."

As we went in the house, I went to flip the light switch up only to find out our electricity had been disconnected. Daddy didn't pay the bill again.

"Someone reported that you kids, are always here by yourself so as we go to investigate, we learned that your father got arrested this morning for selling narcotic to an undercover cop, so you kids need to come with us, Mrs. Long stated. All I could think about was momma and how sad she would have been to know all of this was going on. Momma and now Daddy are both gone. Now Calvin and I were about to be lost in a whirlwind of shit. We stayed in the system until they got a hold of Aunt Melissa, people call her Mimi.

Calvin was about to turn 15 years old and I was 13. We hadn't heard or seen Aunt Mimi until she showed up to take us out of there. We went to live with her and was so glad that she came to rescue us from out of that place. The entire time Calvin made sure they didn't split us up. He raised so much hell the people never put us up for adoption until Aunt Mimi came and took us both.

When we got alone with Aunt Mimi, Calvin screamed out,

"What took you so damn long? My momma was there for you! We just knew we had you, Aunt Mimi!"

She looked over to Calvin and me.

"I'm so sorry. I had to get things together for myself before I could take on the responsibility of two more kids." I was confused.

"Two more kids?" I looked at Calvin and from his facial expression, he was wondering the same as I.

"Yes." She looked back over to Calvin

"Boy, I have my own problems to handle!" Aunt Mimi didn't look like the Aunt Mimi we knew. She appeared very tired and stressed. She started crying about how Shirley (our mother) shouldn't have left her in this mess. Calvin and I looked at each other in confusion, once again we both were thinking the same thought...*As if you were in the same shit we just got out of.*

'What!!' was the only look we could give her right now. We found out a lot of things we didn't know about Aunt Mimi, like she had a set of twins. We never knew that she was even having a baby, let alone twins.

"Where were they? How old are they? What's their names?" I asked.

We're now living with Aunt Mimi and her messed up

situation. When we got to the house Aunt Mimi introduced us to her man Tyrone. My first impression of him was that he looked weird. He was standing there in the foyer with this cunning look on his face. Like he wanted to eat me or something.

The twins were two pretty little girls. They were so happy to see us, like they knew us already. I asked them their names. *Misery and Pain*, they said sadly. I thought that was so evil to give them nicknames like that. But when I learned that was their actual birth names, I shook my head in disbelief. Who, in their wrong mind would name any child, Misery and Pain? Hell, even in the right mind, you wouldn't do that. But hey, this is Aunt Mimi we're talking about.

Misery looked like she just finished crying or something.

"I'm not calling them that!" Calvin said laughing out loud which made me kind of chuckle.

"Me neither," I smirked.

"Call them what you want because I can care less," Aunt Mimi stated. All I knew was that if she's like that towards her children, we don't stand a chance of any salvation in this house. She showed us our spots we'll be sleeping at but not before going over her rules and regulations toppled with the do's and don'ts of her house. In my mind, I told myself we are about to learn what hell really feels like.

Aunt Mimi knew how to clean up when the social worker came around and she sure knew what to say to keep the money coming in. I never saw her spend any quality time with the twins. She leaves the cleaning and feeding to me. She only plays the mommy role when she's either entertaining, high, or crying from a beat down courtesy of her man.

I found a corner in the room I shared with the twins. I would write in my journal about all the things I had to see while trying to figure out how to get from under all this mess. I could never talk to Calvin because he was in and out like dad used to be. He would come into my room from time to time to see how I was doing and if I needed something but that was about the full extent of our communication day in and day out.

"Calvin where do you be going?"

"Why?"

"Because I hardly ever get to see you anymore? Only in passing. Why? Is daddy not coming for us?"

"Sis, I can't be here and see the things that goes on in here and be good with all that."

"Calvin, I know that it's a lot for you to deal with especially being here, but it's better for me mentally that I know where you are, ok?"

Calvin always gave me some money and told me to hide it in a good place, so whenever I needed to use it for something I'll have it. I knew what my brother was doing. I just never said anything because I knew he was not going to listen to me and right now he is the only family and friend I have. Aunt Mimi never questioned Calvin's where a-bouts. She heard what he was doing from talk on the streets. So, she told Calvin he either pay his way or get out. So, Calvin paid her to shut her up, so the people wouldn't come and put us in the system again or even take her twins away. As I wrote in my journal, I start to write a poem to my Momma.

IF ONLY YOU COULD HAVE...

If only you could have

stayed around a little longer.

If only you could have

been much stronger.

If only you could have

fought through the pain

If only you could have

held on to see me soar

before you entered Heaven's door.

If only you could have

Then maybe we should have

Shared and talked about life more.

If only you could have

Then maybe you would have

Prepared me for your call.

If only you could have

I know you would have

Stayed around for us all.

Serina Garland

My Aunt Mimi was the one who had her shit together once upon a time, until Tyrone came into the picture and got her doing stuff she never did before. He always was saying things to break her down, like she wasn't shit and useless. He had her selling her things, stealing from stores, not to mention selling drugs to get money for him. She was even using drugs herself. He did everything he could to break Aunt Mimi, although I think she was already broken. She never seemed to care about anything not even her babies. She shoved them away from her every time they came near her. Calvin couldn't stand seeing Aunt Mimi like that, because she was not the same Aunt Mimi that we so adored and loved. Calvin couldn't get along with Tyrone at all.

Aunt Mimi used to be so beautiful and had her head on right. Calvin could not believe that she went down like this. I often wonder if it was because momma died. They were both like Bonnie and Clyde. Aunt Mimi was always around her. Then she disappears after the funeral. We didn't see her until she came for us.

Calvin stayed away from her as much as he could. It wasn't like she showed any concern or cared about us kids or even had our best interest at heart. The people from the children's service just gave us to Aunt Mimi without even questioning her or anything. Calvin and I got lost in the system just to be put into another one.

I decided to sit down on the bleachers before going home to play 'mommy' to the twins. I was so upset because I didn't know what to do for the girls or myself. I didn't want nobody to find out what was going on at home, either. Then they would have wanted to come and take us all away and split us up. Calvin would never forgive me for telling the people our living situation and what we were enduring. He told me to never tell anyone about what goes on in Aunt Mimi's house because they would take the twins too.

When I got home, I heard Aunt Mimi yelling at the girls to be quiet! They both were hollering and crying at the same time. When Aunt Mimi heard the door open, she yanked me into the house by my shirt collar. Immediately, she started yelling at me.

"Where the hell have you been! You know these girls needed to be picked up from school by a certain time!" You could literally see spit flying from her shouting mouth.

"I'm SORRY Aunt Mimi. I had a project I had to complete."

"I don't give a fuck! You better have your ass there on time to pick them up!"

"What? Why is it my responsibility to do your job...again?" Why did I say that? The next thing I knew, I was seeing stars and lightning. She had smacked me right in the face so hard it sent me stumbling backwards. I caught myself from crashing onto the floor. I wanted to hull off and punch her right in her shit, but my momma taught me better than that. The next time she tries doing that again, I'mma have to pull out my 'beat a hoe's ass card!'

"Now get these girls out of here and get them washed, fed, and ready for bed." Aunt Mimi sashayed her ass over to the couch where Tyrone was flopping down next to him. I looked at her and rolled my eyes, but not before catching Tyrone smiling slyly winking his eye at me. I then grabbed the twins by their tiny arms and took them in to take a bath. I wondered who took care of the girls before I came.

I never called them by their given names because I couldn't believe Aunt Mimi would name them that. She had to have been high or depressed about their father to do something so sinister to her own children. Who calls their child Misery and Pain? I call them Jewel and Diamond.

One day while Aunt Mimi was in one of her better moods, I got up enough nerve to ask her what made her name her beautiful babies, Misery and Pain. She looked at me with so much hurt in her eyes.

"Carla, that's a story I prefer to take to my grave." I could see the tears forming in her eyes. She said nobody listened to her then and the depression just got out of control. I couldn't make out what she meant by that. So, I asked her was it ok if I called them something else.

"Carla, you can call them whatever you want. I don't give a

fuck so just leave me alone." She became agitated and pulling on her clothes. So, I knew what that meant... she was ready for a hit.

"Why our mommy yell all the time? Diamond asked me one day. "Why don't she ever play with us?" Goes Jewel.

"You mommy is just in a lot of pain and as soon as she gets better, she'll show her love more and spend more time with you.

"Carla! Am I one of mommy's pains? Is that why she calls me Pain?" I had to fight back my tears.

"No, Diamond. You nor your sister is the reason for your momma's pain. She had problems and pain way before yall were even born." My heart was ripping up inside.

"Aunt Mimi will get it together soon and she'll show you two her real love." The girls looked at me.

"Carla, we love you."

"I love my Diamond and Jewels too." I said to them rubbing both of their heads. The girls had a bath, ate, and then I put them to bed. I got my journal and started to write another poem.

Serina Garland

MAMA

I don't know what to do!

I'm confused on this thing called Life.

Would I ever get it right? Or would I crumble or should I fight?

Mama! Mama!

I don't know what to do.

Why? did you leave me in this mess, is this all just a test? For the

hurt inside won't let me rest.

Mama, Mama!

I call you. But! you don't answer. Are you there? Can you hear me, do

God even hear my prayers?

Mama, what should I do?

I'm trapped in this place called hell, I want to scream and yell. How!

What! To who can I tell

Mama what do I do?

I cried myself to sleep, afraid of life's up's and down's Never

knowing what to expect. Wishing I could turn back the hand of time.

Where my life was full of laughter and smiles. Knowing that you

would be there. To wipe away my tears. Helping me through all my

fears, keeping me safe, sheltering me, loving, and caring for me.

I miss you mama; I miss my friend;

I will love you forever! There will be no end.

You are my special friend I will always hold deep within my heart.

I will be empty, lost and lonely without my Friend, but I know

You are in a special place where God needs you to be.

Mama! Rest In Peace.

Enjoy your wings, but remember that I won't stop asking myself...

Mama! Mama!

Where are you!?

From, time to time.

Serina Garland

As I was finishing in my journal, I heard some voices screaming and hollering in the living room. I tiptoed out to see Aunt Mimi and Tyrone fighting over who got the last hit on the pipe. I knew Aunt Mimi did drugs. She was being secretive about her stuff. But now her secrets are spilling over.

Now, she doesn't care who sees her anymore. I guess she got tired waiting for us kids to disappear out of site, while Tyrone does him. They were so into making sure the other one didn't get the pipe that they didn't even notice I was standing there. I eased my way back to the bedroom wondering why they're fighting over a pipe and why the hell they only have one? I shook my head because I really didn't care to find out either.

I checked on the twins while wondering what Calvin was doing. I called him but he did not answer. I pray for him every night to be safe on these mean streets. I often wondered where he laid his head at night, right before crying myself to sleep.

The next morning, the twins and I woke up to Tyrone coming from out of the bathroom with his pants halfway off his butt. He looked over to us with his glassy eyes.

"What y'all looking at?" We stopped in our tracks. He grabbed me by my arm pulling me closer to him.

"You sure is pretty," he said greedily pulling me closer to him and brushing up against my breast. I yanked my arm away from him and I pulled onto the twins then ran into the bathroom quickly locking the door behind us. Jewels was frightened.

"Why did he do that?" she asked.

"He's scary," said Diamond. I had to have the talk with the girls. They were five years old now and they needed to know the three no's. I remember when my momma had that talk with me. Not because I was in any danger at home, but she said that I should know these things.

I told the twins that if anyone touches them on their tot-tots, privates or bottom or touch and do anything like that to them, it's a No No!

"Run and tell me or an adult." Jewels started crying.

"What's the matter? What's wrong?"

"Carla, Tyrone touch me there."

"Touch you where!?" She pointed to her private part. I was afraid to ask what she meant. I hope that dirty bastard didn't put his nasty private part in her.

"He touched me Carla down there. He touched it and said he want some of that. What did he mean Carla?" I continue to tell them that no adult is to ever touch you. You yell, run, and tell somebody. They both said 'ok'.

When we finished getting dress, we went into the living room.

"What the fuck!" I screamed out. Aunt Mimi was on the floor naked with Tyrone on top of her having sex. Diamond called out for her momma. Aunt Mimi nonchalantly yelled for us to get out of there. I grabbed the girl's stuff and we left. I shook my head in shame because her daughters were not her priority and they didn't seem to have precedence before her man.

Now here's Jewels telling me that Tyrone molested her which means Diamond was touched as well.

"What was mommy doing?" Diamond asked full of fear. I just began to sing the ABC song with them to take their little minds off of what they just saw.

"Carla I'm hungry," Diamond stated. I was so thankful that my brother had dropped me off some money because I wouldn't know what to feed the girls let alone myself sometimes.

I took the girls to McDonald's to get some breakfast right before school. As we sat at the table eating our breakfast, people kept stopping at our table to say how cute the girls are and always asking if they were twins. One lady stopped and said "You both are such pretty little angels and well behaved too. What are your names?" Diamond started to say Pain when Misery shouted out "Diamond and Jewels!" Such beautiful names for beautiful little girls. I bent my head in fear of the questions that were coming next. Jewels asked the first question.

"Carla! What does Misery mean?" I was so hurt with what she asked me and tried to find a way to answer such a harsh question for such beautiful girl.

"Jewels, Misery is not the word for you, and neither is Pain for Diamond. That's why I call you girls my Diamond and Jewels because you are rare precious pieces.

"Yeah! But what does it mean?"

"Jewels, it's when a person has unhappiness and discomfort in their life that they are so out of control with their emotion".

Diamond said, "Carla! Why can't the teachers and kids call us Diamond and Jewels"?

"They don't know to call you that yet."

"That's what I call you girls."

"We don't like it when the kids call us Misery and Pain. Can you tell the teacher to change our names and to call us Diamond and Jewels?"

"I will ask her if it would be ok to call you girls by your nicknames."

"Ok! Ok!" The girls shouted as I cringed in my seat over the black cloud Aunt Mimi placed over their heads with those cursed names.

I prayed that the questions were over. Never thought I would have to be the one to answer these questions though. Once we got to school, the girls started shooting questions and demands at me.

"Carla! Carla! Ask Ms. White. Ask her. Ask her."

So, I obliged.

"Ms. White, would it be ok if the class and staff could start calling the girls by their new nicknames, Diamond and Jewels? They are having a really hard time trying to understand the horrible names their mother gave them.

Ms. White smiled and said that would be great for us all. I kissed Diamond and Jewels and left for school myself.

As I was heading to class, I ran into Terrance and Tori. I looked at them in amazement because I never seen them before at school. We all had such big smiles on our faces because we were happy to see one another.

"How we y'all doing?" Both Terrance and I looked down in shame. Tori didn't even have to wait for us to explain.

"I know," she answered as if she knew our plights. The bell rang and we all went to class, but not before agreeing to meet each other on the bleachers later.

When class was over, we all met in our spot over at the bleachers. We all were smiling and so excited to see each other, that we all started to talk at the same time.

"Ok, ok, you guys...breathe. What's been going on?"

Terrance began shaking his head blowing all his frustrations out of his mouth.

"Ladies first."

"Well, my story hasn't changed much," Tori began. "My

mom is still getting played by her boyfriend, Victor, every day, and it doesn't seem to bother her like it does me," she said.

"What do you mean?" I asked.

"Well for one! Her so called man Victor is playing my mother like a fiddle. She acts like everything he says is true and that he won't or wouldn't lie to her. She seen him touch another woman and then had the audacity to say she was sorry!"

"What?" Both Terrance and I said at the same time.

"I don't know what to do to help my mother see that Victor is such a Taker. All he does is take, take, and take!"

"Well," I started. "My aunt Mimi is so messed up on drugs that she doesn't see anything good about life. That's why she chooses to let her boyfriend Tyrone, who is supposed to be her man, lead her down a path of destruction. He is her breaker and he's not just hurting her; he's hurting all of us. I had to answer questions from my twin cousins that no one would want to answer."

"What was that Carla?" Terrance asked.

"The girls asked me why did their mother name them Misery and Pain."

"Wait, wait, wait. What?" Tori couldn't believe what I was telling her.

"Is that their real names? Like really on their birth certificates like that?"

"Yes, but I call them Diamond and Jewels. And they love it! They ask me to see if the school can call them that instead of those cursed names."

"Well, my mother can't see she is being played by her man name Ray who is, by the way, taking her for a ride. It's just something about this dude I can't put my finger on it yet. I hate him with a passion!"

"Well, guys...I don't want another run in with Aunt Mimi, so let me go pick the girls up on time from school to keep the peace at home for all of us."

"Yeah, I feel you Carla," Tori said as she continued.

"Let's meet up again soon guys and let's figure this stuff out and try not stress so much about it. Let's see what we can do to make us happy. This is our year! So, let's accomplish our goals."

I picked up the girls and we headed home. As we were walking, we ran into Calvin. I grabbed and hugged him so tight and so did the twins. We all shouted his name out at the same time.

"Calvin we miss you!" He said he was on his way to the house to see how we were doing so, we all walked to the house together.

"How you been sis?" My face suddenly changed to sadness.

"Things are very bad at Aunt Mimi's."

"She doesn't do anything for the girls and Calvin they are starting to ask questions that I don't know all the answers or what to tell them half the time." He immediately became angry and worried.

"Calvin, they asked me why their mother named them Misery and Pain?" He just shook his head.

"They know we call them Diamond and Jewels, right?"

"Yes, they know, and they love it but they still have questions."

As we were getting closer to the house, Calvin gave me a roll of money and told me to please keep it out of Aunt Mimi's reach and sight. Of course, I agreed. When we got inside the house, Aunt Mimi looked at Calvin with hunger and thirst written all over her.

"Hey boy! You got something for me?"

"...and hello to you too Mimi." Calvin shot back refusing to acknowledge her as Aunt Mimi and just calls her Mimi instead.

"Oh yeah. Hi baby!" Aunt Mimi knew that she could not rub Calvin the wrong way because he will leave without giving her anything. Diamond ran up to her.

"Hi mommy, how was your day?"

"Girl move out the way and go do your homework or something." She was scratching and sniffing at the same time.

"Mommy, what's wrong?" Diamond asked caringly. Aunt

Mimi pushed her out of her way.

"Pain, move and go somewhere. Can't you see I'm busy." I called Diamond and told her to come get something to eat.

"Diamond?!" Aunt Mimi loudly burst out yelling.

"Who the hell is Diamond?"

"Mommy, that's me."

"I didn't name you no damn Diamond. I named you Pain and the other one Misery. Who told you your name was Diamond?"

"Mommy, Carla always called us Diamond and Jewels." Quickly, I jumped to their rescue.

"Aunt Mimi, it's just a nickname I call them."

"I didn't tell you to call them that damn name! Now did I? They are just what I named them...Misery and Pain. I went through the torture of having them bastards. If I can turn back the hand I was dealt, I would've chosen a winning hand."

"Aunt Mimi!" Calvin yelled. "Cut that shit out or I'm outta here!" I just looked at Calvin and walked back into the kitchen.

"You see that rude bitch? How could she say that stuff to those girls!" Calvin was infuriated and told me to just walk away. Aunt Mimi was getting ready to come at me when Calvin grabbed her by the arm.

"Yo, Mimi! You need to stop this shit. What's wrong with you? I didn't come here for this!" She looked at Calvin and calmed down. Calvin reached in his pocket and pulled out something showing it to her. And on cue, she was all smiles. Calvin told her that if she wants this to keep coming in, she better not touch me and to let the girls enjoy being called Diamonds and Jewels.

Once she got the money and stuff, her demeanor changed with a wicked fake smile stretched across her face.

"Boy! You know I was just playing with them girls. Everything's good here baby." I guess Aunt Mimi was out of her mind. She didn't even remember that we had this conversation about me calling the girls Diamonds and Jewels. She sure was cool with it. That was a moment in time when Aunt Mimi was good and wanting to chat. I tried to find out where she came up with the names for the girls, but she just changed the subject.

Calvin came into the room and asked us if we were ok. I told him we were fine and that I don't want to be here anymore, and I think about running away from here but I don't have any place to go.

"Carla please, don't talk like that. I need you to hold on. I'm working on something and I can't do it worrying about you," Calvin said.

"But Carla if you leave what's going to happen to us?" Diamond had overheard us. Diamond was the outspoken, observant, and the one with the "why" questions. Jewels was more laid back, quiet, but wise at the same time. Calvin assured us all that things were going to be ok. And we need to be good and stay out of Aunt Mimi's way.

"Girls, I'm outta here I'll see you all soon," Calvin said.

"Calvin wait! I have something for you," I yelled out. I pulled out a gift for my brother. Today is his birthday, March the 3rd.

"Carla you didn't have to do this." He opens his gift and smiles. It was a chain that said, "*Big Brother.*" Calvin was all choked up and said he loved it and that he won't take it off.

Now I have a little something to remind me of my baby sis. It's close to me. "Carla are you still writing?"

"Yes, Calvin every chance I can."

"Good, keep it up Sissy! I'm waiting for that book". We both laughed then Calvin left, but not before running into Tyrone.

"Hey big man!" Tyrone said. "How the hell you doing man?" Calvin just looked at Tyrone and shook his head. He knew that Tyrone was not good for Aunt Mimi and that he keeps her high and disconnected from life. He made it his business to come around when she had money and got her check from the Agency. He always knew to come right on time and when I was around too, to give Aunt Mimi her cut. The next day she's broke and Tyrone is kicking her ass. All he do is take.

I took the girls in the kitchen to fix us something to eat. In comes Tyrone. High and touchy. He grabs Jewels and says,

"Hey little mama." Jewels jumped and ran over to me. Diamond said, "leave her alone." Tyrone looked at Diamond and laughed.

"What did you say Ms. Pain?" Diamond screamed really loud "THAT'S NOT MY NAME! My name is Diamond." Tyrone laughed.

"Your momma said she named y'all Misery and Pain."

"Tyrone why? Why are you bothering us?" He chuckled.

"Oh, I haven't bothered you yet", he said with a cunning look in his eyes and a smirk on his face. Then he left out of the kitchen.

"Carla I don't like it when he's here," said Diamond.

"Me neither," Jewels whispered. I agreed with them both.

"Let's just try to stay out of their way," Jewels said especially when momma be acting like she's seeing things and looking funny. We all laughed.

The next day, I picked up the girls and we went home. When they got there, Aunt Mimi was high as a kite, staring up at the celling.

"Hey mommy, what you looking at?" Both the girls said, but she never moved. I told the girls to just go in the room. Aunt Mimi was stuck in a place of her own, right now. Her thoughts of being here were gone. I often get this sad feeling upon me because I can't seem to reach her. I often wonder where she goes and what she's looking at. I smile at the thoughts in my head.

When we open the door, Tyrone was laying on my bed with his hand in his pants.

"Tyrone! Wake up this is our room, please leave!" Tyrone woke up and smiled at me and told me to come lay down.

"Tyrone please leave my room." He jumped up and grabbed me by both my arms and pushed me down on the bed. At this time Diamond and Jewel were yelling and screaming for him to let me go. I reached for the vase that was near the bed and hit him over the head. He jumped up and ran out of the room holding the side of his now bleeding head.

"YOU WILL BE SORRY FOR THAT BITCH!" I grabbed the girls and we embraced each other and just sat there and cried. I couldn't or just didn't want to believe that Aunt Mimi would have this fucking pervert around her girls. She didn't even come to see what all the yelling and screaming was about. I thank God for watching over us every night. I was afraid to leave out of the room but I couldn't believe that I had that strength in me that I never knew I had before. The word *AFRAID* woke up something inside me. It's my acronym for never letting anyone have me afraid again. Almighty, Father, Release, All Inequities of the Devil . A is for ALMIGHTY F is for FATHER R is for RELEASE A is for ALL, I is for INEQUITY and D is for DEVIL, so that I will protect them from all evil seen or unseen. It's a good thing that we stopped at the store before coming home and got a bunch of junk food. That was our dinner tonight. I'm still in shock that Aunt Mimi was so zonked out that she didn't even come to see what was going on. I just couldn't believe that the twins and I were not safe at home.

The girls ate their candy and did their homework. So, to pass the time away, they sat quietly watching TV as I told them about our upcoming venture to Tori's house tomorrow just to get their little minds off of what just happened the day before. I told them to use the pail if they had to go pee-pee or just hold their poo-poo for in the morning. I started to write in my journal.

AFRAID

Have you ever been afraid?

Afraid of what lies ahead of you?

Never knowing that the person you knew would ever be a threat to

you.

Now he's the one you're screaming STRANGER DANGER to!

What do you do?

Who do you call?

What is this all for?

I need to stand tall. There's no one here to hear my calls.

For this woman right here, is lost inside her own mind.

I must fight every attacker that comes my way.

I can't!

I won't let this cat allow me to be afraid.

I will be the overcomer.

I will stop this abuser, this rapist, this attacker, who's lost in his own

head injecting pain on others.

Don't let your emotion stop you from fighting your battles.

God got you!

Even if you are AFRAID.

When, morning came we went to Tori's house. After our day at Tori's house, things seemed to go left for us all. We started to see less and less of each other. The CTT group had went they own way. Everybody had their own problems that we needed to work out for ourselves. We all were trying not to put too much on each other.

I took the girls to Mickey D's. While they were eating, I called Calvin to see how he was doing.

"Sis, I'm good I have some great news to tell you and I hope you will be as happy as I am right now," he said. I am so very happy. So, I couldn't wait for the next time to see my brother. He was too happy so for me to tell him what Tyrone just did, would rock his world. I just have to stay aware and always be alert of Tyrone. I have to watch out for the girls and myself.

When we got home, Aunt Mimi was having a card party and the house was so cloudy and fogged up with so much smoke and people. I bet Aunt Mimi didn't even know half of these people. I never seen any of her friends come over. So, I guess these were all of Tyrone's riff raffs.

"What is that smell and why are all these people here?" Jewels asked. I just walked the girls past the crowd and into our room only to find that there were people in the room doing their own thing.

"Get out of here! This is our room!" I yelled. Aunt Mimi

came down the hall high as a kite, she told them to get out and go to the front. Aunt Mimi shocked us all with just her presence being there. We were so use to her being zonked out somewhere and Tyrone running her house. However, she had her reason. She was just being nice to me, just to ask if I had seen Calvin. The party seemed to last all through the night I was so thankful that tomorrow was Sunday. The girls went to sleep. I sat in the corner writing in my journal. I dozed off and fell asleep. I jumped up to Tyrone standing in front of me holding his dick in his hand.

"Are you crazy!" I yelled! "What the fuck are you doing?!? How did you get in here?!? Get out of here Tyrone!" I was praying that Aunt Mimi would hear me and come to my rescue, but that never happened. Tyrone told me to shut up! Before I wake up Misery and Pain.

"I just want you to touch it just touch it, that's all Carla."

"Tyrone if You don't get the fuck out of here I'm going to scream to the top of my lungs." Tyrone started putting his penis back inside his pants. As he jumped and ran the hell out the room, I jumped up and locked the door behind him. As I turned around, Jewels and Diamond were staring at me. They both asked at the same time.

"Carla what was Tyrone doing in our room?"

"I hope he wasn't trying to fight with you again." I told the girls that they need to stay out of Tyrone's way, and always try to stay together. The next day Aunt Mimi was sitting at the kitchen table. She looked like she was just sitting there thinking.

"Hey Aunt Mimi, how are you feeling this morning?"

"I'm doing fine," she said. "I have been trying to call that knucklehead brother of yours and I haven't gotten an answer back from him yet." I sighed, I wanted to let Aunt Mimi know what Tyrone has been trying to do. Aunt Mimi noticed a worried look on my face.

"What's wrong with you, Carla?"

"Aunt Mimi I miss my Momma. She would have protected me from anything." Aunt Mimi looked at me.

"Protect you from what Carla! Well!" This was my chance to say what was on my mind while I had Aunt Mimi's full attention.

"Well for one thing, she would protect me and your girls from Tyrone."

"What the hell are you talking about Carla? Protect you from Tyrone for what?"

"Well, Tyrone has been making advances at me, he tried to rape me and he has been touching the girls." Aunt Mimi jumped up and was now face to face with me.

"No! No! Carla I don't wanna hear this shit! Tyrone is not doing no shit like that!" Something must've penetrated her motherly instincts. "When, Where, and Why the hell didn't you tell me!"

"Well! You was right here in the living room, spaced the hell out. He finds time to do what he wants when you are high. The other time was when you was having a party I am so afraid for the girls right now."

"Carla! don't tell me that right now. I can't do this! Not right now! I can't handle this shit right now! Call your brother, and see if he will answer the phone for you and leave me alone. I need to process all this shit!" I thought to myself *process* this? Wow. While your creepy boyfriend was trying to molest me and is looking at your girls sideways, and all you can think about is where is Calvin, so that you can get high and be spaced out again?

I went into the room with the girls, got them dressed and we went to the park. I started looking for my brother on every street corner that I thought he would be on, he was not there. When we got to the park the girls went to play and I tried to call Calvin again. This time Calvin answered.

"Hey baby sis, what's up?"

"Why haven't you been picking up your phone? I really needed to talk to you Calvin!"

"About what? What's wrong Carla? Calvin this is not something that I want to talk about over the phone. Not while the girls can hear me right now."

"That's cool Carla. Let's meet up at the house. I want to

talk to you as well."

When I hung up the phone with Calvin, my thoughts were all over the place. Now I wanted to know what Calvin wanted to talk to me about. At that same time fear set in and I got scared, with the thought of what my brother's reaction would be when he finds out what Tyrone has been trying to do to us. I don't want my brother to get in any trouble for me, let alone Tyrone.

Me and the girls stayed at the park half of the afternoon before heading back to the house. When we got to the house, Tyrone was there and Aunt Mimi was sitting there with him, like I never told her anything about him this morning. She was so Jittery and adamant in trying to get whatever he had. She stopped when she noticed that we were looking. She told us to go to the room. I gave her a look that made her say get out of my face. I hurried up and pushed the girls to the back. We went in the room I locked the door. We were in the room for several hours before Diamond said she was hungry. I turned around to Jewels but she was asleep. I guess she was so tired after her day at the park. Me and Diamond went into the kitchen to find something to eat. Tyrone was still here looking at TV. Aunt Mimi was over at the window staring out into space again. I never understood why Tyrone and Aunt Mimi were together in the first place. They never really did anything as a couple, besides getting high, or Tyrone coming for money or when Aunt Mimi didn't have any, she had to sell something, or go out and get some. I never knew what she did out there, but she always came back home with some money and drugs. Tyrone would be right on her heels. I couldn't understand why Aunt Mimi let Tyrone break her down like that. That's not the same Aunt Mimi that lived with us. She had fire in her. Tyrone always had Aunt Mimi begging for something. He always putting his damn hands on her and she always seemed to forgive him. Aunt Mimi is not an unattractive woman, she just needed to leave the drugs alone and get her shit together.

I found something to make for the girls to eat. I was so busy preparing the food that I never notice that Tyrone was not in the living room. Aunt Mimi was still sitting in the chair at the window but this time she was staring down the hall in a daze. I didn't think that Tyrone would try anything while we were up moving around and Aunt Mimi was in the room with us. I continued cooking us something to eat. Diamond and I started singing *I Will Always Love You* by Whitney Houston. When all of a sudden we heard Jewels screaming. I turned around so fast, ran to the back. I didn't even notice that Aunt Mimi wasn't in the living room staring up at the ceiling or out the window anymore.

She was on top of Tyrone stabbing the shit out of him. As she was stabbing him she was saying "Get off of me, get off of me. I won't let you do this to me again!" Jewels ran over to me.

"Carla why was Tyrone trying to put his thing in me? I

felt him pulling my legs open. I woke up and he was on top of me. Mommy came in and started stabbing him with the knife, yelling not again! Not again! What is she talking about Carla?" I had to grab Aunt Mimi.

"It's ok Aunt Mimi! Its ok."

"No Carla! He's not going to hurt me or anybody else anymore!"

Tyrone was laying there bleeding to death. Calvin had just arrived.

"Where's everybody at?" I ran to Calvin with tears in my eyes saying there was something wrong with Aunt Mimi, she just stabbed Tyrone. Calvin went in the room to see what has happened and got Aunt Mimi off the floor. Aunt Mimi looked like she was in a trance. Calvin called the police and ambulance then he asked us what happened. We all tried to tell him what happened at the same time. Calvin had to tell us to calm down again.

"Carla what happened here?" I began to tell Calvin that Tyrone was trying to rape Jewels and tha he's been trying to rape me. I never thought he would try the girls especially with all of us in the house."

"What Carla!" Calvin said, "Why didn't you tell me this shit!"

"I didn't want to worry you, but that's what I was

calling you for." At that time the ambulance came to attend to Tyrone and the police was right behind them. Aunt Mimi was rocking back and forth she just kept saying get off of me, get off of me. I looked at Calvin to ask what is she talking about, and Calvin hunched his shoulder as to say he don't know. The police asked us what happened and Jewels said "He was on top of me and mama jumped on him with a knife and started yelling *not again*! And she just started stabbing him and crying get off of me."

The ambulance put Tyrone on the stretcher and wheeled him out. The cops handcuffed Aunt Mimi as she was still in a state of confusion. She just kept saying get off of me, get off me! Calvin asked them where were they taking her. One of the officers came over to us and said that she seemed to be having a breakdown so they were going to take her to the psychiatric hospital so that she could be evaluated. Then we could go from there. The officer asked if we lived there. Calvin said that the twins and his sister lived here. I was just stopping by to see them.

"Well! we are going to have to report this to the children services and let them look into it. For now, is there a family member they can stay with right now?" Calvin said yes really fast.

"My Aunt will take them in."
The officers had to get a name, and Calvin gave them Diane Blackwell and her number. Calvin was smart always thinking on his feet. He sure knows how to think quick and smart under

pressure. Before the cops came, Calvin was on the phone with someone telling them what had happened. So I assume they got the heads up that they might get a phone call. So when the officer called Ms. Blackwell she was already ready to say yes. So the officer said that they would bring us over there. Calvin said officer if it's ok, he can drive us there. I didn't even know Calvin had a car. The officer thought about it and said ok.

"We'll check up to see if they are there and make sure things are good. We will tell the children services so they can link up with you guys." So, they left and I had so many questions for Calvin.

"Who is this lady? When did you get a car? What you think they going to do to us, or Aunt Mimi?" Calvin looked at me and said Carla can you give me a chance to answer the first question. Calvin said that Ms. Blackwell is Dana's mother.

"Who's Dana I asked?" Calvin smile. "Dana has been my girl for over a year now."

"How come I'm just hearing about her then?"

"That's what I was coming to talk to you about. Ms. Blackwell is her momma and she takes in foster children. She is a nice woman Carla and I think, No I know, that you and the girls will be fine there. Aunt Mimi is going through something and it's more than just what happened here today. It was a snap that was coming and was way overdue. I pray that this is a release on what she's been fighting with for a long time."

After all of the cops and detectives and people that were taking pictures left, Calvin Told us to go an pack a bag. As we were riding to Ms. Blackwell house, Calvin started to tell me about Dana and how much he really loves her.

"How come this is the first time I am hearing about this Dana? If you loved her that much why did you keep her a secret?"

"Carla, it wasn't like that at first but there's something about Dana that makes me want to do better. Before I met Dana I was slanging drugs on every corner. I did what I had to, to get money to keep me afloat as well as you guys. But Dana came into my life and she seen a better me and told me that I was too good to be doing what I was doing. So, for the last year when you thought that I was still on the corner, I was working Carla. I have a job now that I'm proud to go to every day and I get a paycheck that I earned." Calvin then paused for a second before continuing.

"When I thought about what I was doing Carla and how I was supplying Aunt Mimi with something that was tearing her apart, I didn't think about the girls or Aunt Mimi or even you Carla. That was not how I wanted Aunt Mimi to fight her demons. I listened attentively then replied,

"I hear you Calvin! I'm so proud of you. We cannot let Aunt Mimi go down like this. Something is seriously haunting her. So, we have to make sure that they don't throw her under the bus.

You know how the system works. Calvin, we haven't seen daddy in four years and he never even tried to reach out to us. I wonder every day if he even knows where we are, or even care what we're going through."

We arrived at Ms. Blackwell's house and Calvin introduced us to her and Dana.

"Hello girls," said Ms. Blackwell. "How are you guys doing today in spite of everything that just took place?" We all said fine. Ms. Blackwell looked at the twins and asked each of them their name?

"And what is your name?" She said pointing to Diamond who started to say Pain then shook her head.

"I'm Diamond and this is Jewels." She looked at me and I told her my name is Carla. We stayed at Ms. Blackwell house for about a week when the social worker came to take us away. Ms. Blackwell talked to the social worker.

"What do I have to do to get all of them to stay with me?" The tall lady then answered.

"You will have to fill out paperwork and we'll have to access the situation before checking to see if you still qualify. But at this time, we need to take them into custody." The girls started to cry saying that they did not want to leave.

"Where is mommy?" Diamond asked. " I want my

mommy?" Jewels cried out but the social worker took us with them. All I could think about was not again. This is like Déjà vu.

"Carla you be strong and don't let them split you guys up. Ms. Blackwell will get you all back," Calvin stated.

Calvin

"Dana, I have to go and check on my Aunt Mimi to see what is going on with her case and see what I can do for her. She is my aunt and the girls' mother and she don't deserve this." I continued pondering the thought of what went wrong and when?

"Dana something is wrong with her and I have to help her." When I arrived at the precinct, they had me talk to a Mr. Tucker. From what I can see, he seems to be a nice gentleman. He told me that my aunt was sent to a rehab place for her drug use and mental health. Did you know that your aunt was raped as a teen?"

"She was what!?" I said. "No! By who? Well that's her story to tell. Tyrone Hunter will recover from his wounds and will be prosecuted for his crimes by the state. He did not want to press any charges against your aunt. I thought to myself *as he shouldn't.*

"Can I at least go see my aunt? Mr. Tucker gave me the address of the facility where Aunt Mimi is at. When I arrived at the facility they told me that Aunt Mimi cannot have any visitors at this time.

"Well, when can I come back to see her?" They told me in 21 days.

"Can you at least let her know I was here?" They agreed .

Carla

I tried to keep us all together but they had to split us up. The girls had to go with their age group and me with mine. I grabbed the girls and gave them a big hug and whispered into their ears. "Do not let them separate you girls. We will all be back soon."

As I was sitting on the bed that they assign to me, I was thinking about Aunt Mimi, Calvin, the twins and even Ms. Blackwell. She really is a nice lady. I even grew to like Dana for my brother.

I stayed to myself at the group home spending most of my time writing in my notebook. I was wondering how the girls were doing. I got a letter from Calvin letting me know that Ms. Blackwell is doing what she has to, to get us all out of that place. He told me that he got as much of our stuff that he could get and put it in storage for us. When the landlord found out what had happened he put Aunt Mimi out. That was fast and something he's probably been wanting to do for a long time. Aunt Mimi was always behind in her rent because of Tyrone. I guess he never knew what Aunt Mimi had in her until that happened to him.

We stayed in the group home for two long weeks before Ms. Blackwell was able to get us. I was so happy to see her and my brother. When they came and got me, I ask where are the girls?

"Carla, we're going to get them too." I was grinning from ear to ear when he said that. I gave Ms. Blackwell a big hug and thanked her so much. When we went to get the girls, they were sitting in a corner holding onto each other. Soon as they seen us walk in, they came running over to us asking us, when are we coming to take them out of this place.

"This place is not a nice place. They keep calling us Pain and Misery, and all the other children just laughed and teased us. Jewels told them what our names were and the counselor said to everybody that was not our names that's on our paperwork.

"Well little ladies, you girls you won't have to worry about this place again, so always remember the beautiful names that your big cousin has given you," Ms. Blackwell said so calmly.

"Are we leaving?" Diamond asked. Ms. Blackwell and I nodded yes.

"Yes! I'm glad we are leaving. They always found something wrong with us and we never did anything."

Ms. Blackwell sign all the necessary papers and we left never to see this place again. By the time we got out of there, school was over and we had about three weeks left before this all happened. I pray that I made it to the 12 grade and the girl's made it to the 3rd grade. Especially with us having to endure so much and to hear that we would of have to repeat our grade, would've been a disappointment.

"You know what sweetheart? Calvin and I went to the school and explain what was going on and that we would not be able to finish out the school year. They felt for everyone and passed you all to the next grade." I was so happy. I had good grades to make it to my senior year and the girls were smart enough to make it into the third grade not the second. Good thing they took their S. O. L's before all of this stuff happened.

"Where's mommy?" Jewels asked.

"Yes, where is she? I want to see my mommy." No matter how mean and uncaring Aunt Mimi were to them, the girls loved their mother. When we got to the house we sat the girls down and told them that Aunt Mimi is getting herself together so she can be the mother they need. The girls went to the room that Ms. Blackwell set up for them. Calvin started to tell me about Aunt Mimi and where she was and that we would be able to see her next week. He told me that Tyrone is in jail and that they did not bring any charges against Aunt Mimi because she was just protecting her children. I was so glad to hear that she was going to be free from Tyrone and that now she can get herself together and work on whatever it is that has her trapped within her own mind. I tried calling Tori and Terrance and neither one of them answered the phone. I wanted to see how they were doing and tell them all the things that happened to me since we last spoke to each other.

It was so different being back at Ms. Blackwell house. The girls were adjusting fine and were so happy to see us all together again. Ms. Blackwell spent a lot of time making us all feel at home. She always seems to find time to talk to all of us either together or by ourselves.

Calvin and Dana appeared so in love with one another and she always kept my brother smiling. It has been three weeks and Calvin was so anxious to see Aunt Mimi. I couldn't wait to see how she was doing in the rehab and if she was getting her mind right.

Calvin came into the room.

"Are you ready to go?"

"Yes," I replied back with a big smile on my face and with joy in my heart that we were going to see Aunt Mimi. After everything that's happened to our mom and dad, Aunt Mimi was the only family we knew and we had to stand by her side because she was always there for us when our mother wasn't around.

When we got to the facility, they escorted us into a room to wait for our aunt to come in. When she entered the room, she looked like the beautiful non stress Aunt Mimi again. She really looks so beautiful. Calvin ran up to Aunt Mimi and gave her a big hug and she just started crying. When we sat down Aunt Mimi asked about the girls, Calvin told her that they are doing well as expected, but they keep on asking for you.

Aunt Mimi started off apologizing.

"Calvin and Carla, I am so sorry for my behavior. I was so lost when Shirley died. I didn't have anyone to talk to or help me stay on the right track."

"Aunt Mimi what made you start using drugs?" Calvin said getting straight to the point.

"Calvin, I was hurt and was so confused and then I was about to be a mother to not one but two babies at the same damn time. I didn't know what I was going to do."

"Aunt Mimi, why didn't you just go back to your mother's house?" I asked.

"Carla, it wasn't that easy. My pain came from me being at her house. Your grandmother, my momma, was not a passionate, or caring mother."

I was baffled. "Why you say that Aunt Mimi? That's your mother." Aunt Mimi looked at me and then to Calvin.

"This has been a conversation that is way overdue and I need to tell you guys my story." Aunt Mimi took a deep sigh then grabbed onto both me and Calvin's hands. I knew that whatever she was about to tell us was going to probable be a shock to our central nervous system especially with all that we've gone through in the past 60 days.

"Well, our daddy had died when your mother had just turn 13 and I was four years old. We didn't get a chance to even grieve over his death. Our mother didn't waste any time getting married again. That's where Leroy came into our lives. Your momma didn't like him and she used to always say she can't wait to get old enough to leave this house. It was a mess at our house.

Everything that Leroy said, our mother would believe him, "over us." It was as if she didn't love us anymore. I fought everyday with the thoughts in my mind, whether she loved us at all or not.

Calvin interrupted Aunt Mimi's story.

So, who's the twins father?

Aunt Mimi didn't want to answer that question.

"Calvin, I'm just learning to process that one."

"Why, Aunt Mimi?" Aunt Mimi quickly grew sad in the face and tears started to roll down her cheeks.

"What's wrong Auntie?"

"Leroy rape me and I ran away and came to my sister's house."

"What? Are you serious?" Calvin stood up in anger for a couple of seconds before sitting back down.

"And where was grandma when all of this was taking place?"

"My mother came home and when she opened the door, she saw Leroy on top of me raping me. Do you know what she did?" We were both scared of the answer.

"She turned around and walked right out of the room! I screamed for my momma to help me, but she never came to my rescue and Leroy never got up until he was finished raping me."

Calvin and I was in a frozen state. Then she continued.

"I laid there in a puddle of blood just crying. I got up enough strength to make it in the bathroom. My mother came in and the only thing she could say to me was to get out of her house! I said mama did you see what Leroy just did? My mother's response was even more sickening. She said she didn't see anything. Just a "fast ass bitch" that wouldn't stop flaunting herself at her husband. She screamed for me to get out of her house! I was standing there with tear's rolling down my face and I said again to my momma, why? Where am I supposed to go? This woman who is supposed to care and love me said that was not her problem."

"That's when I came to you guy's house. I never knew I was pregnant until it was too late to do anything about it. Shirley convinced me to keep it. She said that she would be there for me.

Then Shirley, my sister, my best friend died and I was all alone again. I couldn't help you kids because I didn't know how to help myself. When I saw your grandmother at the funeral, that just opened up a can of worms that spun me out of control. I wandered around like a lost puppy. Sleeping wherever I could, with people I just met. I ended up in a shelter and then out of the blue, I went into labor. I never had prenatal care nor any ultrasounds. When I gave birth the only name I had was *Pain* because I had so much pain in my life. The thought of having his baby made me sick to my stomach. Then the doctor delivered a devastating blow to me when he said here comes the other one. I never knew I was having twins because I never went any doctors appointments. When the other baby came out, I just named her Misery.

"Why? Aunt Mimi why?"

"Because those were the only names that went with the hurt, pain, and misery I was feeling at that time, Carla. Now that my mind is clearer and don't hurt as much because I'm learning how to deal with it." Aunt Mimi dropped her head down with tears dropping onto the table. After wiping both her eyes, she continued.

"Now! I can focus on what I did to my girls and myself. The shelter was the help I needed at that time because they assisted me in getting back on my feet. They help me find an apartment for me and the twins. Then about a year later, Tyrone came into the picture. He made me believe that he was going to take care of me and the girls, but he never cared for them at all. He started beating the shit out of me and started breaking me down piece by piece and the next thing I knew, I was back doing things I wasn't proud of. I was neglecting my girls, leaving them with his high ass, so I could sell my body to get him his drugs. He gave me just enough drugs just to shut me up."

I wouldn't have ever imagined Aunt Mimi going through all of this torture. As much as I didn't want to hear anymore, I knew she wasn't finished.

"Once I was hooked, I couldn't control my urges. My story goes on and on. When Tyrone was doing this to my girls, I snapped. I knew I had to protect my girls from what I had inflicted upon them. I was so out of it you guys. I just hoped my girls can one day forgive me."

"They will," Calvin stated. "They love you too much. In spite of how they came into this world. They love their mother." I couldn't help but notice a piece of paper she was holding in her hand.

"Aunt Mimi, what is that paper you been holding in your hand?"

"Oh yeah! Can you please give this to the person that is taking care of the girls? Can you tell them that I love them and I'm so sorry for how I treated them?"

Calvin looked at the paper Aunt Mimi was holding. He took it and handed it to me. Aunt Mimi had the girls name changed from Pain Daniels to Diamond Re'nay Daniels and from Misery to Jewels Ta'nay Daniels. She kept the names we called them. When I saw the document, I jumped up and hug her. The director came in and told us our visit was over for today. We hugged Aunt Mimi one more time and told her how we're so proud of her.

On our way home Calvin talked about how proud and happy he was of Aunt Mimi and he was so glad that she is working on herself so that she can get things in order for her girls.

"Carla, I'm ready to settle down with Dana. How would you feel if I asked her to marry me?"

"I would love that Calvin. You know whatever makes my big brother happy, makes me happy. I just have one question, though?"

"And what's that sis?"

"You don't feel that you two are too young right now?"

"No, because I truly love her. She completes me."

When we got back to the house, the girls were watching TV. Ms. Blackwell had settled them down for the night.

"How was your visit with your aunt?"

"It was great. I'm so glad that things are working out for her. And that she's learning how to fight her demons."

I grabbed a glass of water from out of the refrigerator and went to my room. I laid back across the bed and started writing in my journal. I was so happy for Aunt Mimi and so thankful to God for watching and keeping her from all her demons.

As I thought about My Aunt I couldn't imagine all the things she had to carry at her age. I wrote another poem for this one really brought the tear's out.

LET IT OUT

Let it out little black child

Let out your sorrow and pain

Express those feelings that you have bottled inside.

Let out that Misery and Pain

Let it out little black child

Let out what upsets you, so you can heal.

Let it out my little black child.

You will go through your tests, even go through your trials. You will

shed a few tears or even scream out loud. BUT!! It's ok.

LET IT OUT

My little black child.

Let your tears began to fall. Release that sadness you hold within.

So that the grieve you have will decrease, And the JOY!! Will spread

beyond your limits.

The next morning the girls were up eating Cereal. When they saw me they both started jumping up and down.

"Carla," they both said at the same time, "when can we go see mommy?" All I could say to them was soon. I have to ask Calvin to check into that. Dana came into the kitchen at this time and greeted us all. She sat at the table with a cup of coffee and asked me if I would like to come shopping with her.

"Yes! I would like that. Then the girls chimed in.

"Can we come?" Dana smiled and looked at them.

"How about I take you girls somewhere special on another day? Let Carla and me catch up on getting to know one another." The girls agreed but with such sadness.

Ms. Blackwell came in all bubbly like she always is and told the girls that she was taking them to get some clothes and shoes today. The girls jumped up and down, before going to get themselves together.

"Oh, Ms. Blackwell...before I forget. My Aunt Mimi wanted me to give you this piece of paper that has the girls new name changed legally." She smiled as I handed her the piece of paper.

Me and Dana left right after that and took the bus downtown. Once we reached the place she wanted to sit down and talk. I already knew what she wanted to speak with me about.

"Carla, I want to talk to you about your brother," she began. "You know I love him with all my heart. He asked me to marry him and I want to know how you feel about that."

"Well Dana, all I want is for my brother to be happy and do the right things. I see how happy he is with you Dana and how you turned him around. I'm so glad I don't have to worry about him being on those corners anymore. I know he really loves you Dana, but I do have some concerns of my own."

"Like what Carla?"

"Well for one thing, don't you two feel that you are pushing to get married too soon? Like, what's the rush?"

"For starters, I'm not pregnant so let's get that out in the opening. Yes, we are young. That's why I told your brother that I think we should be engaged for a while first and let's see where this will take us. And he agreed."

Dana and I then left the food court after we ate. As we were leaving, I ran into Terrance who was working in the food court. I smiled so hard when I saw him. He came from behind the counter and gave me a big hug.

"Terrance, you work here?"

"Yes and I still work at the warehouse too. I just needed another income Carla."

"How is everything going with you? How is your mom?" I asked while staring deeply into his darkness behind his eyes.

Terrance sighed. "Carla, that is a long story to be told for another time." As much as I wanted to pry, I decided this was not the right time nor place. Terrance hugged me again and went back behind the counter.

"Carla, I will call you. I promise. We need to talk," Terrance said. So before leaving I asked about the crew.

"When was the last time you spoke or seen Tori?"

"I haven't had any time to see or talk to her. What about you?"

"No, I haven't had a chance to catch up with her either. Things with me have gone haywire. We all really need to get together and soon." I told Dana about Terrance and Tori and how they were my only friends.

When we got back to the house Ms. Blackwell had something to tell me.

"The director from the rehab call to see if your Aunt Mimi can have a visit with the girls next week."

"I think that would be really good for them". She agreed.

"They're always asking me a lot of questions that I do not have the answers for. I do not know too much about you all's story and only what they told me and what I got from all of you."

Ms. Blackwell had such a mothering effect on you. You just have to love her. Weeks went by before the girls got to visit with their momma. They were so excited and talkative that they kept asking us a lot of questions on what should they say?

"Do you think mommy is going to show us any love because she never did before." Mrs. Blackwell interrupted.

"Your mother wasn't in her right mind at the time, I think that she is doing so much better now so let's just give her a chance to see how she is handling things and how you girls receive her, ok?"

When we got inside and got the girls situated they brought in their mother. When the girls saw their mother they both ran up to her and gave her a big hug with her hugging them so tight. Aunt Mimi started to cry because she felt that she was never there for the girls. Once she sat down with them, she looked at them both kissing them softly on each of their cheeks.

"You two are so beautiful! I can't believe that you are my babies. I am so sorry that I wasn't the mother you guys had needed. Mommy was in a dark place and I had so much hate in my heart and I took it out on my babies. There is no amount of words that I can say to make you understand how so, so, sorry I am."

"But mommy, you called me Pain," Diamond said sadly. Jewels jumped in.

"...and you called me Misery."

"Was I a pain to you mommy?"

"No baby! And neither was your sister misery to me.

Your mommy was just so lost. I didn't even know who I was. The first thing I did when my mind cleared and I was able to understand what I did. I change your names from Misery and Pain to Diamond and Jewels. You both will keep these names forever. Miss Diamond Re'nay and Miss Jewels Ta'nay, I love you girls. You both are my babies. I'm so, so sorry! Can you ever forgive me?"

The girls Jumped up and gave their momma a great big hug.

"Mommy, we never stopped loving you. You will always be our mommy."

The girls had a great visit with their momma. I never thought that I would see that much joy on their faces. Just being able to get their momma's undivided attention. Aunt Mimi looked so well, and without stress. I am so happy for her.

Aunt Mimi then asked Ms. Blackwell if she could take the girls to get something from out of the vending machine so that she can speak to me.

"I'm so sorry that I was not a better Aunt to Calvin and you. You guys don't know how much it helped me to let out to you guys all the pain I held inside. Carla, I now see where my hurt was coming from. I really was lost in my head. I know this is gonna sound like a broken record, but when your mother died, that was it for me. My sister was the only one I could talk to. She knew how your grandma was and Carla it wasn't easy for me living with your grandma. Once daddy died, my mother became so filled with hate that she took it out on me and your mother. That's why Shirley couldn't wait to leave. I hated that she left me there, but she never stopped checking on me. Carla it's hard to talk about my childhood. However, I feel you are old enough to know this and my counselor said it is good for me to let it out. This is the hardest thing that I've ever had to tell people about, but this program has been such a blessing to me. It has truly help me get from behind my darkness and face all my fears, my hurts, and my pains. I couldn't breathe Carla, but now I can exhale." Ms. Blackwell and the girls were still at the vending machine while the twins fought over what they wanted. Aunt Mimi continued.

"They teach us in here to talk about the things that had us lost and out of control. Things that made us hurt ourselves. They teach you to channel it into something positive that would help you to make a better you. The first thing is for us to acknowledge what have happened to us and ...well Carla, I really couldn't and wouldn't except that my babies were my mother husband's kids."

"When my momma witnessed this monster she called her husband, raping me and did nothing to help me, my soul and innocence would be lost forever. I still can't believe how she just walked out Carla." I looked at Aunt Mimi with tears in both our eyes.

"But why didn't Grandma help you?"

"I don't know Carla. That day my love for my momma was lost forever for me. Like I said before, when she came back in my room, I couldn't believe the words she shot out to me. *Bitch! I told you to stop wearing those hot ass shorts around this house!* She blamed me! She said that's how you intimidate these men out here." I looked at her with disgust written all over my face.

You're my mother! You are supposed to protect me! I'm the child. Why? Momma why you allowed him to do that to me and not help me!

"Carla, do you know what she said? She told me to get my fast ass out of her house! I cried and said where do I supposed to go? She said I don't give a fuck where you go! I just sat there with this dumfounded look on my face. Leroy walked in and patted my mother on the butt. Then to ad insult to misery, she had the audacity to turn around and kiss that man on his lips. He looked at her and asked what's going on in here, like he didn't just rape me. Your grandmother had the nerve to say *nothing honey.* He grabbed her by the ass and said, well let's get it on and just like that, my momma left. She left me there crying, bleeding and in pain. Carla I could go on and on about my life in that house. I was so blessed to have a sister that loved me. So, when she died I was devastated. They tell us in here that it's good to talk about our pain to others that we know we have inflicted pain upon. So,

Carla whenever we can have these talks please understand that I need to just let it out."

"Aunt Mimi, you can talk to me anytime you want. I'm so sorry you had to go through that. We're family Aunt Mimi and we are here for you."

Ms. Blackwell returned with the girls just in time to hear the end of our conversation and said to Aunt Mimi that she just wants her to get herself right in her mind, so that she can be there for the girls because they love their mother and need her more now than ever. Aunt Mimi hugged Ms. Blackwell and thanked her for being there for us all. I know that God sent you our way. The girls cried because they had to leave their mama again. Aunt Mimi assured them that they will see her again.

When we got back to Ms. Blackwell house, I went into my room and wrote in my journal. Our life at Ms. Blackwell house was so peaceful. I had all the time I needed to write in my journal and catch up on my school work. The eleventh grade came fast and it left just as faster.

I remember sitting at the window thinking about Tori and Terrance, wondering what they were doing when my phone rung and it was Terrance. He sounded so sad, but I was happy to hear his voice.

"Hi Carla, Tori is on the line as well."

"Hey Tori."

"Carla it's been so long for us all," Tori said.

"Carla, Terrance wants to tell us something together."

"Ok Terrance, what's up?" Terrance proceeded to tell us why he called.

"Y'all know you two are my best and only friends. I have to let you know that my mother died Monday and I was arrested and put in jail."

"What!?" We both said in sync.

"Terrance what happened? Why are we just hearing about this?"

"I just found out she passed away on Wednesday, the same day I was released from jail."

"Terrance! What happened? How did you, of all people, wind up in jail?"

"To be honest, it's a long story. We have to find some time to talk, but right now I have to help plan a funeral for my Mama. Carla, I also wanted to know if you could write one of your poems for me?"

"I certainly can Terrance. No problem. I'll get right on it."

"Will you be there too, Tori?"

"Terrance you know I will. Let us know all of the details and we'll be there."

"Hey, girls I'm going to end this call but not before we make a pack to meet up with each other. There is so much I need and want to talk about." At the same time, we all shouted "CTT."

"We are there!

After hanging up with them, I was feeling some type of way with tears running down my face. Ms. Blackwell knocked on the door to tell me I can eat if I like. She seen me crying and asked what was wrong.

I told her what I just found out regarding my friend and how sad it was to hear about my friend's mother. It just brought flash back of my own mother passing away.

"My friend wants me to write him a poem about his mother to be read at the funeral. I never got a chance to know her."

"Well," Ms. Blackwell said, "Carla you are a good writer. Write what you feel from the heart." Ms. Blackwell kissed me gently on my forehead then told me when I'm ready eat, my plate will be in the microwave.

Serina Garland

I THOUGHT! I WOULD HAVE YOU FOREVER

I thought! I would, have you forever

Never knew you would go so soon

A part of me left that day when I lost My Mama "

I can't believe that I will never see that smile

Upon your face again.

I thought I would, have my mama forever. Never thought you would

leave me so soon.

My heart is empty my tears are full.

I'm losing.

You have given me more than you would ever know

Just by being my mother."

I thought I would have the honor of asking,

You to walk me down the aisle.

I thought you would hang around, to continue our talks,

to explore our plans, or even

Hear my children's giggle.

The hardest thing for me right now,

is knowing that I won't see my mama.

How can I let you go?

I thought, I would, have you forever.   I know

God has gained an angel.

I will always cherish the memories we had.

Until we meet again.

Sleep in Peace Mama, I will always Love you,

Forever my Queen. Forever My Mama ...

The next morning, I woke up to the girls jumping up and down excitedly on my bed because they were going to see their momma again today. I'm so happy that the girls are getting to have a real bond with their mother. Aunt Mimi has so much more mental control now. I'm so glad that she found the help she needed. I'm sorry but not sorry that it had to happen this way. Tyrone was a dog and he needed to be exposed for all the stuff he put us through, especially Aunt Mimi.

 At that time Calvin came in and the girls went from nagging me to asking him a bunch of questions.

Diamond started in first.

"Calvin, we're going to see mommy today."

Calvin smile. "Yes, I know. I'm going to take you girls to see her soon."

"Calvin? I been having scary dreams at night. Is Tyrone coming here when mommy gets out?" Jewels asked with a nervous and shaky voice. Calvin sat the girls down on his lap and begin to explain to them as best as he could and hope that they would understand.

"What Tyrone did was bad and no one should have to be hurt like that. Tyrone hurt your momma and he tried to hurt both of yall. What you did, Jewels, was good by screaming loud enough so someone could hear you and stop him. It could of went wrong but, God had all of you guys covered that day and for the rest of y'all days.

"Yeah, but what is mommy going to do? Is she going to let him come back?" Diamond asked with fear in her.

"No, no. You don't have to ever worry about him. The police put Tyrone in jail behind what he did to you baby and no man or woman should ever abuse one another, especially a child."

"That was wrong how he treated mommy. Calvin, why was mommy so distant sometimes?" Diamond asked.

Mommy was sad Jewels said, but she's happy now. She laughs and play with us too."

"Yup Jewels said and she changed our names to the beautiful ones that Calvin and Carla calls us.." Diamond was ecstatic over their now permanent names.

"I hated being called Pain," Diamond said with Jewels adding in. "...and I hated being called Misery!" Jewels roared".

"Girls, when you get old enough to understand maybe your momma will tell you the story behind your names, but until then, just enjoy your new names and being beautiful young girls."

"Alright y'all? Let's get it together so we can hurry up and leave." We quickly got ourselves dressed and was ready to go see Aunt Mimi. Ms. Blackwell stayed home this time and let Calvin take us so he could visit as well. When we got to the visiting room, the girls were so happy to see their momma. They started shooting questions after questions at their momma. The questions were coming so fast that Calvin had to tell them to slow down and let her answer some of them. Aunt Mimi looked at us with a look that told us it was time to answer some of their questions.

Diamond continued with her interrogating questions.

"Mommy, why did Tyrone do bad things to Jewels?" Aunt Mimi explained.

"Baby, Tyrone was sick and he messed with the wrong mother's child!," goes Aunt Mimi causing all of us to burst out in laughter.

"Calvin told us that he is in jail, is that true mama?" Diamond asked.

"Yes Diamond and I pray he's going to be there for a very long time."

"Mommy, why was he so mean to you? And why you was always looking up at something invisible?" Diamond asked.

"Baby, momma was very sick and I was so lost at that time. I often wondered why myself." Aunt Mimi's words were ripping at my heart, not to mention the tears dripping from her eyes didn't make my heart or soul feel any better.

"I knew God was up there and maybe, one day, He'll come down to help me!" We all bent over in laughter. But I'm back now and ready to love all over my Diamond and Jewels.

Aunt Mimi asked the girls to go play with their toys while

she chit chat with Calvin and me. Aunt Mimi began telling Calvin and me that a lawyer came to see her about Tyrone and told her that the state was taking on this case and he is looking at years for attempted rape on a minor.

Calvin said, "As they should.." Aunt Mimi looked over to him with such a worried look on her face.

"Yes, but there is more."

"What Aunt Mimi! What?"

"Well, for starters, the group's program director told him my story and about the girls and they want to do a DNA test on Leroy so they can build a criminal case and arrest him for what he has done to me."

"They told me that under the statutory law, he can still be charged for raping me and if the DNA test prove that he is the girls' father, which he is, he's gonna be looking at a lot of time in prison as well. As I said before, my life at my mother's house was awful and she never protected me from Leroy. He used to touch me in inappropriate ways all the time and my mother never said or did anything about it."

"Calvin, like I told you guys, she even walked in on him raping me, but instead of helping me and beating his ass, she turned a blind eye and walked out. When she came back in the room I was laying there crying and bleeding all over. She just said get the hell up and clean this mess and when you done you have to find somewhere else to go. No comforting me, no baby I'm sorry. Instead, she screamed at me to just leave!

That's when Shirley took me in. I didn't even know I was pregnant, until it was too late to have an abortion. I was so skinny from being stressed out. Shirley convinced me to keep *it* and not give *it* away. She said that she would be there for me and help me take good care of it. I never knew that she would leave me alone to handle this all on my own. I thought she would be there to help me raise these guy's and we would all do it together." Aunt Mimi was on a nonstop loose lip battle as she resumed with the story stuck on repeat.

"When I saw my mother at the funeral with him, I lost my everlasting mind. I really went off the deep end and my ship was sinking fast. When I finally gave birth to Pain I didn't know what I was going to do. Then when the doctor said here comes another one I thought they were playing a trick on me. They laid both of those babies on me and said here are your beautiful babies. All I could think of was the pain that this man put me through. Now, I have two of his seeds staring me in my face every day all day and all I could see was the misery and pain I had to endure when I looked at both of them."

"Well Aunt Mimi, you have us now and we have each other. Let's work on getting better and doing what you have to, to find your inner peace, so you can move on from all your pain. The system will get Tyrone and Leroy for what they did. They messed up everybody's life," Calvin stated.

Our visit was coming to an end.

"Aunt Mimi, how long do you think you will be here?" She shrugged her shoulders. "I'm not sure. I just want to get myself right in my head so I can be a good mother to my girls.

The next day was Terrance's mother's funeral. Tori and I decided to go together. I told Tori how Terrance wanted me to read the poem, but I told her of my feelings about my own momma and I don't think that I could read it without crying hysterically. Tori said Carla I understand and if you want I can read it for you. I hugged Tori and thanked her so much for being there for me.

When we got to the funeral, Terrance was sitting up front. We told him of the last-minute change and the reason for it. He smiled and nodded and said he was ok with the changes.

When it was Tori's time to read the poem. I never seen Terrance cry. I know he'd just lost his momma, but I couldn't believe how much that the poem touched him as well.

Tori and I went back to his godmother house to greet people that came to show their last respects. After Terrance came back from the burial, he was so glad to see that we were still there.

"I knew that I picked two good friends and I thank you for being here for me. Carla your poem was so good. It really touched my heart and I needed to hear those words. Thanks so much my friend," Terrance said.

We stayed with Terrance throughout the day until everyone left. We sat there and talked for a long time and told each other what we all have been going through. Terrance told us what happen with his Mama and how he ended up in jail. Both Terrance and Tori were so surprised that the girls and me had to go into children services and was shocked to hear about Jewels and glad that Aunt Mimi is free from Tyrone and is getting herself together. Tori told us that things are still the same. Her mother is always working, and still dealing with Victor, but he doesn't come over anymore.

"I'm still the 'momma' to my siblings and still can't find time to get into my drawings. So, I put that on hold." Terrance told Tori to please promise him you just won't give up on that. We talked some more and promised each other that we would spend time with one another more this year because last year we fell apart and we went our separate ways. It shouldn't have taken a funeral to bring us together again. But it is what it is. We would always remain the CTT forever. We realize that it was time to go, so I called Calvin to see if he could pick me up and drop Tori off.

When he arrived, we drop Tori off. Calvin and I talked

about Aunt Mimi, the girls, and how things were good at Ms. Blackwell's and how much he loved Dana. I love my brother and I knew that someone would fall in love with him. He is so much like our mother. He is so lovable.

"Carla I know that I'm young and that Dana and I should make sure that this is what we both want, but Carla I truly love her. She reminds me of our mother. She is so sweet and loving and she compliments me in a way that set off value to me. We've been through a lot 'lil sis but through this all we are still here with each other," Calvin said.

"Yes Calvin. I don't know what would have become of me if I lost you too. Dad just totally left us for dead. What happened to him after momma died? Why couldn't he take care of us. He's our father Calvin."

"Well, Carla there is something else I have to talk to you about. What is it Calvin?"

"Carla, daddy was afraid to be alone. Momma kept him grounded. When she died our daddy died that day too. He was so lost and lonely without her that he felt he couldn't be of any use to us. So, he wandered around like a lost puppy trying to get it together but he couldn't. He found himself doing so much stupid things that he just didn't care about anything let alone us."

"Calvin, that's a cop out. He was the man of our family and he threw us away. Anyway, Calvin how you know so much about daddy and his issues because you were in the same mess I was in?"

"Well, Carla that's what I'm trying to say?"

"What Calvin, what is it?"

"Umm, I...I've been in touch with our father for a while now."

"What! Why Calvin!? He's nothing to us. Carla I learned to forgive him and I want you to forgive him too."

"What!" I screamed out.

" Hell No!"

"Carla, listen to me. We all lost something when momma died. Look at what happened to Aunt Mimi, the girls, you, me, and daddy too. Carla he went through it as well. I'm not saying what he did, was the most responsible thing to do, but we don't know his pain. We both, baby sis has been blessed to get out of this shit. I know Carla I have or I could be in jail too, just like dad. Instead of me doing better I became angry and rebellious about everything and started doing what I saw. I thank God for Dana every day because without her stepping into my life, I know I would still be slinging drugs. That's what was killing Aunt Mimi and making life unbearable for you girls."

"Well, Calvin I'm not ready to let go of how I feel about dad yet."

"Ok Carla, that's understandable because all I want is for

you to just think about it, ok?"

When we got back to the house, Ms. Blackwell was sitting in the living room with a paper in her hand. She told us that they want the girls to come in for a DNA test. Lord these babies 'dun been through enough!" Ms. Blackwell said.

"They been through so much already and how do you shelter them from what's about to be unleashed?"

"We have to have a talk with them and tell them some things. I feel the questions coming now," Calvin expressed.

"When is this supposed to take place?" He asked.

"The letter says, Tuesday at 10:00 am. So, I have to leave them out of school that day. You know they not going to like that. They are so happy to be in a different school where the kids would never know that their names were Pain and Misery. They are so happy to have friends now and adore their names. They are call the ruby sisters and they love it. Second grade has brought them out of their little shells. They have put all the horrible things they had to endure behind them. Now this! How do we explain this!" I was so upset.

The day the girls had to go for their test. I went with them, because I knew that they would ask Ms. Blackwell a lot of questions that she would not be able to answer. The first question was why they not go to school today and where were we going?

"Carla, why are you not going to school today?"

"I want to go with my Diamond and Jewels."

"Where are we going?" Jewels asked.

"Well girl's, with all the stuff we've all been through, the courts just want to do a swab test on you girls."

"A what? What's that?" Jewels didn't know what I was talking about so I had to explain the best way possible to two eight-year-olds.

"Why?" Diamond yell out loud.

Calvin came in just in time to interrupt that question and save me.

"Hey y'all! Don't you girls look pretty today?" He said then winked at me.

They both replied, "Thank you Calvin and guess what? Diamond said excitedly. "We're not going to school today. Carla said we are going to be swab. What does that mean Calvin?"

Ms. Blackwell stepped in. "You girls are lucky because not only do you get to miss a day out of school, but we're also going to all get ice cream after the test is over."

"Yea! Yea! Ice cream!" They both said jumping up and down.

"You see, the swab test is going to be fun. It's just a test to see who your father is." Jewels seemed to not care one way or another especially when she heard those words...ice and cream.

"Oh, ok because we never knew who our daddy was.

Mama never told us anything about him."

That day came and gone and now we have to wait to see what we already knew.

We were ready to go on Christmas and New year's break. I got a chance to see Terrance and Tori. It seemed like we haven't seen each other in a minute, even though we did, but it wasn't on a good note. I was happy to see them again in school and catch up on our talks. We all had so much to talk about.

"Ok, ok," Terrance said. "I know it's been a long time but we all can't talk at once." He teased.

"I know we missed each other and we have things that we want each other to know," he continued teasing causing us to all laugh. But as Terrance said this, it seemed like a deja'vu.

"So, let's start with Tori. How have you been?" Terrance asked.

"Terrance, my drama ain't nothing compared to what has happened with you. Tell us your story first and how in the world you of all people ended up in jail?" Tori couldn't wait to hear this.

"Yes, Terrance please tell us again how that happened? And by the way, I'm so sorry about your momma, but what happened?" I said not meaning to sound so cold and uncaring. Terrance began to tell us his story about his momma and what her boyfriend, Ray did.

My mama had caught full blown AIDS from that punk but

she later found out that he wasn't the one. However, it was my sperm donor who she contracted it from."

"What! Are you serious?" Tori said.

"What did he have to say to you Terrance after he did that to your momma?"

"It ain't nothing he could say. He's fucking dead. She killed Ray thinking that he gave it to her. I don't have any tears for him. My godmother got me tested and I'm good. To top all this shit off, my Mama's sister married him and has a daughter a month younger than me. She's good also, but her Mama has the HIV virus and still living." Tori and I looked at Terrance in such disbelief.

"Well, that's how my life turned out and I went to jail for my Mama because I couldn't let her endure being in jail sick and dying in there."

"Well Carla...what's been going on with you?" I looked at both of them and shaking my head before taking a deep sigh.

"Where do I start? For starters, I went back into the foster care system along with the girls."

"What! Why?" Terrance asked puzzled.

"Aunt Mimi stabbed Tyrone because he tried to rape my baby cousin, Jewels, who was seven-years old and that trigger whatever Aunt Mimi had going on inside her own head. She just kept saying *not again* over and over. They took her to the Psych ward and Tyrone was rushed to the hospital and then straight to jail.

"My brother's girlfriend mother is a foster mother and she took us all in. My Aunt Mimi looks good now and she's working on herself and the pain that took her down a road of 'not giving a fuck about anything'. She's still in rehab doing the necessary steps needed and making it work for herself so she can get her girls back...I pray. But she did change the girls' names."

Tori was confused over someone naming their kids such atrocious names.

"But Carla what made her name them Misery and Pain in the first place!"

"My Aunt had got raped by my grandmomma's husband and had witnessed it all and didn't even help her own child. I guess everything stemmed from the pain and misery she endured in her childhood, and only she can tell her story better than I can."

"Well Tori, what's been going on with you?"

"My mom hasn't been spending that much time with Victor. I guess that's a good thing but she has been working late and I am still taking care of my brother and sister."

"What about your designs and drawings?" I asked.

"All I can say about that is... that's another story. To keep it real, I haven't really had much of a feel for drawing anything lately. My time has been spent going straight home and caring for my siblings."

"Ok, that's enough about my boring life. My question to you guy's is what happened to the CTT," Tori asked.

We were all so caught up on our own life's traumatic issues, that we forgot about each other.

"Well, CTT, we are Seniors this year. What are we going to do different?" I asked.

"Hey, we have the big prom thing this year! Umm, the million-dollar question is, are we going and who are we taking?"

"Well," goes Terrance. "I have a great idea."

"And what's that?" I asked.

"If you ladies will have me, I would like to escort you both to the prom. We should all go as a three-strand thing that can never be broken." I pondered the thought.

"I like that!" Tori stated.

"Yeah that would be cool for us all. What will be our colors?" I said with excitement.

"Y'all tell me?" Terrance said. All I need is just the color theme." He laughed. It really was good to see him laugh again. He's been through a lot. Hell, we all have and we need this time to enjoy our last year of high school.

"I like purple." That's always been my favorite color.

"No!" Tori shouted out. "I like lavender."

"Well, you ladies can wear the colors you like. I got you ladies, I got you. So, prom's done. Colors pick. Date is a rap."

"Wait," Tori was in thinking mode and I could tell.

"Carla, let me design our dresses. Yours could be purple."

"Ok, ok! That'll be nice." I told her. Hell, I was so overwhelmed because I never participated in anything in school. Now I have best friends and I'm going to the Prom. I couldn't wait to get home and tell everyone the great news.

As soon as I got home, everyone was sitting in the living room talking. I looked at them waiting for somebody to tell me what the hell was going on.

"What was going on in here?" Calvin started talking.

"The DNA test result proved that Leroy is 99.999% their father!" So, he did rape Aunt Mimi. I looked at Ms. Blackwell and asked what now?

"Well," she started, "We have to wait and see what the law will do about it." Calvin chimed in.

"All that Aunt Mimi and the girls been through they need to put that scum bag underneath the jail."

"Now Ms. Mimi can start to truly heal," Dana said matter of factually.

A detective went to the rehab house to see Aunt Mimi to inform her that the test proved that Leroy is the father of the girls and that they were proceeding with the arrest for statutory rape of a minor. Aunt Mimi started to cry. She finally got someone to hear her story and believe her about what this pervert did to her.

Her own Mama turned her eyes to what her husband did and kicked her out. Her own Mama called her children bastards. She never showed her any affection, concern, or even cared to help her. Aunt Mimi felt alone especially after her sister died. The detective told Aunt Mimi that she would have to repeat the incident once again in court. So, they can keep him behind bars. He was being arrested as they speak and would appear in court soon.

He gave her his card and said that he would be in touch. Aunt Mimi called the girls and told them that she loved them and asked to speak to Ms. Blackwell.

She asked her if it would be ok to come visit the girls because she was given a pass to visit her family and she only want to see the girls, Calvin, and me. Ms. Blackwell stated that, that would be fine and good for us all. Today was Thursday so Aunt Mimi visit was for Saturday. We all were so excited to know that she was finally coming out for a visit. Aunt Mimi is really doing good and doing everything to make her life better and right for both her girls and herself. The girls were jumping up and down with excitement. Ms. Blackwell was also happy that the little ones get to see their momma.

People don't understand what their little minds are thinking. I know this will be good for them. I was overwhelmed that we all get to see Aunt Mimi outside of the rehab. I got teary eyed on the thought of how far Aunt Mimi have healed. I can see how strong she is now and how she's put all her pain behind her. I see the fight in her. She's trying so hard to get her girls back and undo the pain she caused them. Aunt Mimi said that she feels that she is on top of her pain and she can fight anything that comes against her progress in getting what God has ahead for herself and the girls. I owe them so much. Especially my time. People don't understand how much time means to people. It's something you can't get back. To us it means a lot, to God it's just time.

Saturday snuck in and the girls couldn't wait for their mother to see their room. Nobody had to tell them to clean it up that day. Once the doorbell rung, the girls ran to the door jumping up and down.

"Mommy's here! She's here!" They both hollered out.

"Ok...ok," smiled Ms. Blackwell. "Let me open the door."

No sooner when Ms. Blackwell turned the doorknob, the girls flung the door open.

"it's mommy! It's mommy!" They was so happy to see their mother.

"Mommy, you look sooo beautiful," said Diamond hugging onto her mother's arm.

"Mommy, come see how pretty our room is?" Jewels bellowed out grabbing tightly onto her mother's hand pulling her down the hallway to their bedroom.

"Ok girls, give your mother a chance to get in the door and have a seat first." The lady that was with Aunt Mimi was nice too. She let Aunt Mimi have some time with the girls alone, but not before they asked me was I coming? I know they love their momma, but they still feel sort of protected by me which is why they needed me by their side. At the rehab, they couldn't be alone yet with their mother. That was one of their house rules. The girls began asking their mother so many questions and Aunt Mimi answered what she could.

"Mommy, we love you so much." She had plenty of questions with one main one in mind

"Mommy, why did you call us Misery and Pain?" I could see the tear's forming in Aunt Mimi's eyes as she embraced them telling how lost and broken she was.

"Your mommy was in so much pain and misery that was all I knew at the time. I went through a lot my babies and mommy took her anger out on you girls and the whole world. Every time I saw you girls, all I could see was what I had to endure. Mommy was so trapped in her own pain that I forgot that you were my precious gifts but I had to learn that with a sober head. Now that I'm cleaning up my act, mind, body, and soul, including what I made a mess of." She paused and rubbed each of their cheeks kissing them on their forehead.

"I know you probably won't understand everything

mommy will tell you, but it's time to move on. I never told you girls who your daddy was. I was hurt, confuse, and a shame. I felt dirty, lost, and unwanted." Of course, they understood nothing their mother was telling them. But it felt good to Aunt Mimi as part of her healing process.

"Why mommy? Why?" goes Jewels.

"Baby, what Tyrone tried to do to you was wrong, right baby girls?" Aunt Mimi looked from Diamond to Jewels.

"Yes! And it was scary too," Jewels expressed.

"My mother's husband did that to me and he is you guy's daddy."

"No, mommy. He's not our daddy. He's grandmommy's, husband, right?" Diamond exclaimed as Aunt Mimi nodded in agreement to the latter.

"How come he did that mommy?" Diamond has always been an extrovert and always said what was on her mind, not to mention very advanced. Jewels, now she was the introvert and was the more silent, reserved one yet very observant.

There's a lot of sick people who have no problem abusing others and being mean to them.

"I promise mommy will do all that I have to, to get all of us back and into a safe and decent home.

"Yea! That's gonna be great for us all." Said Jewels.

"Oh, I really would like that mommy. Why did Tyrone try to hurt me mommy and what did you mean when you was stabbing him saying not again, not again?" Diamond continued her mini interrogation of Aunt Mimi.

"Carla said something to me earlier that day that woke something up inside of me and made me feel so ashamed when she told me that she wished her mother was here to protect her. It took me back to the time my mother was there but didn't protect me so I knew that I had to do whatever I had to do to protect my babies. I played along with Tyrone that day I let him think that I was high as a kite. I was high but not the way he always seen me. In all reality I was on point that day. I had to act like mommy always acted to make this man think that I was out of my mind and was not paying attention, but I wasn't out of my mind. I cringe every time I think back on the stuff I let go on under my nose. I get so sick for I was not in my right mind to protect you all. I was too busy taking care of my own habit. When I heard you scream, I took off running. I lost my mind. All I could see was him on top of me. All I seen was what Leroy did to me and that's all the vision I seen and I couldn't let him do that again." As much as I wanted to stop Aunt Mimi from telling the girls this conversation what was well above their mental and understanding, I thought it was best to just let her continue.

"Who is Leroy, mommy?" Diamond asked.

"Leroy is my mother's husband. Remember I told you earlier that he was you guy's father and that I never wanted you girls to know who he was, but I knew this day would come."

But ain't your mommy our Grandmommy?"

"Yes," Aunt Mimi said.

"But why haven't we seen her?"

"That's because after all those bad things that happened to mommy, I left grandmommy's house and moved to your Aunt Shirley house."

"Ain't Aunt Shirley Carla and Calvin's mommy, right?"

"Yes! That was their momma, my one and only sister. Carla always talking to us about her."

"Mommy, I wish we could have met her but why did your mommy let him hurt you?"

"I don't know baby."

"Mommy, do me and my sister have to see that man?"

"No baby, never! When you girls get older and you choose that you want to meet him that will be your choice, but that man would always be dead to me."

"What about your mommy? Jewels said.

"I know that they teach us to forgive and I can forgive but I can't have a relationship with my mother ever again because she did not protect me. I am so glad that God has given me another chance to be a good mother to you girls. I want to take this time to tell you Carla that I am so sorry that I couldn't be the aunt that you guys needed me to be. I've should've taking better care of you just like Shirley was always there for me. My reason for getting you guys was totally fucked up, it had nothing to do with me wanting to do right by my sister at that time. It was so I could, have extra money coming in to support my habit, and have somebody to take the girls off my hands and out of my eyesight at the time."

Aunt Mimi looked at me with tears in her eyes.

"Carla, could you ever forgive me?"

"I was so upset with you Auntie because I was still dealing with the death of momma and I had to grow up fast because I had your little ones looking up to me, so I had to protect them."

"I know Carla and I'm so sorry I put that all on you."

"Aunt Mimi, I'm just so happy that you are getting your life back. "At that time, Ms. Blackwell came in and told us that lunch was ready. We all hug each other. Aunt Mimi pulls both the girls to her and ask them if they understood what she was talking about, and that Leroy is your father.

"We understand mommy. We just want to come home with you!" Both the girls said at the same time.

"Soon," Aunt Mimi said, "soon girls. Mommy working hard on that."

We had a good lunch but it was time for Aunt Mimi to get back. She kissed everybody and said that she can't wait for the next visit.

Aunt Mimi

It was about three weeks since I went to visit my girls. I was called for a visit. I was so excited because I couldn't wait to see my girls. But to my surprise, it was not them and when I saw who it was, I stopped dead in my tracks, turned around and told the director that I didn't want to see that person. The director told me to make your peace within. Then move on.

So, against every hate bone in my body, I went over to face my mother and ask her why was she here, and what did she want with me.

"Hello baby. How have you been doing?"

"What! how have I been doing? Are you serious Joann?" I couldn't believe this bitch had the audacity to not only locate me, but patronize me by asking how the fuck am I doing?

"First of all, I'm fucked up because of you! Second of all, you allowed your husband to rape me. Now I'm going to ask you again, why...are...you...here?"

"Do you know they put my husband, your step-father in jail and he's going to prison if you don't drop the charges." My skin started boiling causing me to almost black the hell out.

"Now why!? Why in the hell would I do that, huh?"

"Baby you know that, that's not what Leroy did."

"Bitch what!" I yelled so loudly at her.

"So, what was it then Joann? What are you calling your husband raping me and you witnessing it then had the fucking nerve to turn around, walk back out of the room and then shut the door?! Huh?" I saw the director stand up but for some reason, she allowed me to fuss and curse this woman out.

" I have two babies from that rapist. Remember the little babies you called bastards. Well, those bastards are your grandchildren and your husband Joann, is *the* Pappy. So now I have to ask you again why are you here? I can't do nothing for you or your rapist husband. I can forget the pain I endure living in your home, however, one day I can and will forgive you, but I won't ever forget the pain and misery I had to suffer by living there. Now it's your turn to go through you're shit alone. I don't ever want to see you again and don't you ever come here again either. Leroy is we're he should be and I hope he rots in there!"

This bitch here had the nerve to look at me utter words that I became numb to hearing.

"Oh, I won't come back here you lying bitch!" Then walked out. I stood there shaking in disbelief on the boldness of her ever thinking that I could or would ever forgive that man. I had to collect myself because for a minute I couldn't believe my own mother who seen this occur had the nerve to think that I would drop the charges yet alone call me a liar and a bitch all in one breath. But then again, I can believe it. I then advised the

Director to place her on a NOT AUTHORIZED VISITOR'S list. The director came and talked to me and suggested that I go and talk to my counselor.

Carla

Everything was happening so fast they were ready to take Leroy to court and they were ready to sentence Tyrone. Aunt Mimi was so overwhelmed because at the same time she was trying to get all her stuff that she needed to get in order so that she can move with her girls back into society and get a nice place for her children to be safe. At this time Christmas came New Year's came and gone.

Now the CTT were getting themselves together for the prom. Tori was excited that the dresses was coming together. This gave her time to get back into what she truly loved. I still want my purple dress," I teased Tori.

"It will be and I still want my Lavender. This now leaves Terrance to decide what color vest he's going to choose to match our dresses. We all couldn't believe that we were participating in something. We all were so wrapped up in trying to work out our own family situations, that we never had time to join anything that the school was having. This gave us all a chance to exhale from the dark secrets we all held inside.

I began to look back on the eexperiences of my ups and downs, my highs and my lows of this extreme ride that I've been on. So, once again...I begin to write in my journal.

Serina Garland

This ride. right here, is a journey. A life lesson that I had to learn. Now, I understand the words to the song, what doesn't kill you make you stronger. I had to learn how to endure these trials, throughout my years. Standing strong on all the difficult roadblocks that came each day. I had to reach my goals and find my own way, I went through many struggles and overcame many obstacles, it seems that the pain was never going to end, but as a child you can't imagine the hand that you're working with. You just have to play it out. I called on my Mama many times only to realize that mama wasn't there anymore, at that moment I remember how she constantly instilled in me to read Joshua 1:9 she would always say to me, that this battle is not mine's alone. I cry now because I get it! I went from 11 years old to an adolescent before, I became a teen. My little mind had to grow and mature fast. Or allow this system to sink me under. Trying to figure out when all this shit would end.

Overwhelmed that I was leaving this mess behind. My emotions were taking over. I cried, laughed, and screamed. I was so excited to see people I knew and love. I wish for this day when someone or something would help me get out of this unpleasant situation. I have to be careful about what I ask and wish for, because that wish just might be another trap. I got out of one fucked up situation just to walk into more bullshit. The hand I hold has two of a kind with three suspects. Now, I have to learn how to play better or run.

Trying to hide my feelings, covering up my pain, looking for help from the only person that I knew love me. I had to realize that he was seriously in pain too! He never showed it, he stayed away from it, but I knew. I put a smile on my face but deep down inside this mess up hand was a doozy. Waking up to the smell of urine n my face. Screaming, for help but no one came to save me. Crawling up in a ball, crying my eyes out, praying for my brother to rescue me, he was not there, so here I go again with another thing to be concern about. I had to stop being afraid and learn how to fight back. I had to put on my big draws and get this thing right. I will never encounter a night of fright again. I will protect these little ones and myself, continually praying day and night. knowing God will work it out. As I look back on this journey I know! that there is a God and through all these storms there's always an angel right by...

It's going on nine months that Aunt Mimi's been in rehab. She's really doing everything she have to do to get her life back and do good by her girls. I went to see Aunt Mimi on Saturday. Aunt Mimi was always glad to see me. She asked me was I alone. I said yes.

"I thought that we could spend some time together. You know, just the two of us." I was glad that I got her back because I couldn't talk to her before.

I ask her could we sit down before we leave.

"Aunt Mimi, I want you to hear my poem on how I was feeling about you at the time." She nodded her head, "Ok Carla. Let me hear it."

"Well, I call this one Angry.

ANGRY

How can you be so consumed with yourself that you forget or

neglect the precious things that God gave you to uphold?

How can you be so lost or stuck within your own Mind that you

forget to help or protect us?

I'm angry with you or with me. I don't know yet.

For your kids didn't matter, nor the sheep that God so entrusted upon

you to care for.

I'm angry because you won't shake this hold that the devil has upon

you.

I'm angry with myself for I'm afraid. I'm trying to cope and protect

the life that belongs to you.

They scream, I scream, we scream, but you're so lost in your own

thoughts you can't even hear us. Do you even care that we are Here?

Aunt Mimi hugged me and cried while apologizing again. She said how sorry she was for she didn't know that I was fighting some of her demons too.

We left and went to McDonald's ate and talked for hours. Aunt Mimi asked me was I coming to live with her when she gets out. I knew this question would present itself when Aunt Mimi was focus. I was ready to answer it.

"I would love to, but I want to go to college and pursue my studies in journalism."

"I think that...No. I know that the girls would love to get to know you better and spend that quality time with their mother," Aunt Mimi said.

"You know what Carla? You're right and I'm so sorry again that I fuck up your childhood with my demons."

"Aunt Mimi, I know, but it didn't kill me it just made me stronger. Now I can go out and get what I want and be good at it. I know now that what God has for me is for me. I don't know how expensive college would be but I have to follow my dreams and give it a try."

"I'm so happy for you Carla and I'm so glad that Ms. Blackwell was there to make all you guy's ending a little better. I thank God for her and how she opened her home for all of you. Knowing that you guy's where there, made my recovery easier. Aunt Mimi was allowed to go out by herself; however, she was given a time to return back. We end our day and she went back to the rehab. I went back to Ms. Blackwell's. Ms. Blackwell greeted me with a warm embrace saying that she missed my presence today. She sure knows how to make me feel good. She asked how was my visit. I like talking to Ms. Blackwell she always seem to have time to talk to us all. It's so comforting in knowing that we are not a burden to her, she enjoy us all being here with her. I know momma would love her. She tells us all the time that we bring her so much joy. She always say how she is so thankful that God had her in the right place at the right time. I'm so happy my brother and her daughter are getting along well. It brings me so much joy to see my brother happy once again. We all been through it since mama died. We were just forgotten about and it seem like we were deep in shit. So through it all Ms. Blackwell was our Savior. She asked me what I was going to do about college. What about the prom. I told her that Terrance asked Tori and I to be his prom dates.

"Both of you?" she asked confused.

"Yes."

"Well, what did you say."

"We both happily said yes even though we have different color tastes."

"What color did you two pick?"

"I like purple and she likes lavender."

"That's pretty together," she said.

"Yeah, but Terrance vest is supposed to match our dresses."

"It will look nice and work itself out just fine. You will see baby," she said.

"What colleges did you pick?"

"I picked the ones where I can study journalism. I pick three, NYU, Temple University, and University of Pennsylvania. I hope one of these school accepts me."

"They will! You are a good writer Carla and I love reading your materials."

"Thank you. I just pray that the cost doesn't hurt me too bad. I put in for some scholarships and had to write an essay on why I think I should be chosen. Ms. Blackwell is always so positive.

"Everything will work out for your good baby, y'all see."

I went to my room to settle down for the night. When I got a knock on my door. In came Calvin. Dana was right behind him.

"Hey sis," Calvin said. "We haven't chat in a while. You about to graduate girl. I'm so proud of you. We had a long road, but we made it on top. After momma passed away and daddy got lock up we had it tough sis! But look at us now. Mama sure was watching over us Carla and she fix everything for us all. Even Aunt

Mimi."

"Yes she did. Calvin momma was always there looking after us even when we thought we were by ourselves."

"I'm so glad I met your brother and that he is doing so well. I'm glad mama was here to help you guy's all stay together you didn't deserve another bad thing happening in your lives," Dana goes.

We all talk for a long time before Calvin said he was tired. So, we all called it a night.

The next morning, I went to meet up with Tori to see the dresses that she drew for us. The dresses were beautiful and she knew a lady that could make them for us.

"She's not going to charge us a lot to make them either," Tori said. But we still wondered what color vest Terrance was going to wear. We were just glad we were going to the prom that it didn't matter. We pick out our shoes to wear with the dresses.

"We have to go next week to try on our dresses."

"Yes Tori, I can't wait to see how it fit". We talked and set up a date to go back to try on our dresses. We talked a little while longer before heading back home. She stopped at the store and ran into one of the girls from school.

"Hi Carla, I never seen you around here before?"

"I just go and come," I said. She asked me was I going to the prom. I didn't want her to know what the CTT plans were , so I just said I might. I couldn't get friendly with others and I know that, have to change. Don't get me wrong I talk to other kids at school just not how I talk to Terrance and Tori. We can relate to each other. When I go to college, I hope I have other good friends.

I took the girls to see Aunt Mimi. They were very excited. As if it was their very first time seeing her. Aunt Mimi had a day pass so we took the girls to the park then to Mickey D's. The girls ask could they go play in the playhouse and we said yes. I asked Aunt Mimi was she ready to take on the girls by herself.

"Carla I'm not going to pretend that it's not going to be scary and a challenge at the same time, but I'm ready to be a real mother to them. I want to give them so much of the love I didn't give them sooner. I know now that they are a victim as well. I have to show them that we are survivors. Carla I can now cope with all the difficult issues I had to experience. I get it Carla when you say what don't kill you it makes you stronger. I'm stronger now to fight against those demons that try to come my way. I'm ready for them in the Name of Jesus! He's my rock and I stand on him Carla. He picked me up from that sinking sand I was in and I give him all the praise."

"I'm so proud of you Aunt Mimi if no one ever told you. I am."

"No! Carla I'm so proud of you. You are graduating girl. In spite of all that you've been through. I'm very proud. I know your mother would be boasting now."

We both smile at that. I asked would she be able to come.

"Can't nobody keep me away. Just make sure I have my ticket."

"I will. The prom is in three weeks."

"You are going, right?" she said.

"Yes! Terrance is taking Tori and I and Tori designed our dresses."

When I got back to the house, I saw the mail on my bed from Penn state and NYU. I was shaking and ran to Ms. Blackwell with excitement and nervousness in my stomach.

I scream, "Look, these are my letters from the colleges". I know that I score a 1600 on my SAT, but I was panicking for I wanted to get into one of these schools.

"Ok, baby open it."

"I can't. Can you open it for me please?" Ms. Blackwell opened the one from NYU first. She said congratulations baby they accepted you. They want to give you a partial scholarship into their school." We jumped up and down. When she opened the other one from Penn State she said congratulations again they accepted you too. She continued reading the letters which said that they are offering me a free ride. We both hug each other and cried . Ms. Blackwell was as happy as I was. She said she knew I was smart.

"You have a gift Carla. Pick one of these colleges and follow your dreams." When we all sat down for dinner. I told them that I made a decision on what school that I was going to. I pick Penn State and I can't believe they gave me a full scholarship. Calvin Jump up grabbing me and hugging the dear life out of me. He said my baby sister is going to college. I'm so happy for you sis. Dana hug me and the twins were smiling and jumping up and down.

"Carla, you get to write in your books there?" Goes Jewels.

"Yes?"

"That mean you are leaving us?" she said sadly.

"Yes and No. I'm going to school to study more on what I want to do, but I will always come back to see you girls."

Saturday Calvin took us to go see Aunt Mimi. She was getting close to getting out and getting her own place for her and the girls.

When Aunt Mimi entered the visiting area, she was happy to see us all. She loves it now that she can spend time and focus on the girls. She told them to let her talk to us for a minute.

She began telling us that she found a beautiful two-bedroom house for them. We were so happy for her news. The only thing I'm hesitating about is I have to show them that I can handle working and taking care of myself and home before the girls can come live with me.

"That's ok, Aunt Mimi. That's ok. Just do what you have to do. The girl's will be alright with Ms. Blackwell."

"I know! I just have a lot to make up for."

"Let's just take one day at a time, Aunt Mimi."

"I can't hold it know more," I expressed.

"What Aunt Mimi?" asked.

"I got accepted into Pennsylvania State with a full scholarship. Can you believe it I am going to college?"

"I am so happy for you. You deserve all good things coming your way just promise me that you will do the best you can and keep a level head. Remember to do all things that are pleasing to God. Never go to a party and loose who you are, never drink out of a cup that you didn't pour or you didn't pop that can yourself. Please baby don't go down the road I went down, just say no to drugs. Just say no! It's not worth it. You will chase behind that first high that you will never get again. That first experience I promise you baby girl you will always be chasing. Just stay straight and stay that sweet Carla that I know and love. I know you will go far. and your mama is Proud, No. I'll take that back. Shirley is looking down and she is very proud of you both."

"Yes she is," Calvin said, "but she's proud of us all."

"Well, the prom is approaching. I can't wait. I'm going to try on my dress tomorrow." I know you are going to look beautiful. Please take a-lot of pictures Calvin because I know you are.

Our visit was over. We went to a restaurant to have some pizza. We ate and talk. Calvin tried to bring up the conversation about daddy again.

"Calvin, I'm so happy right now. Let's not ruin it by talking about him. Not now." We finished eating and on the ride home he started talking about his love for Dana.

I went over to Tori's house so we could go try on our dresses. When we got there the lady just finish the lasts touches to Tori's dress. We both went to try them on and was so amazed on how beautiful they were. Tori really is good at designing. I looked at Tori's dress and said that she looked amazing. She said you look so beautiful Carla. The prom was coming up fast. The day was here to go have a good time, finally. My brother and Ms. Blackwell chipped in for a limousine for us. Tori and Terrance were coming over to my house. So, we all could ride to the prom together. Ms. Blackwell started taking pictures of us. She was so happy for us.

I can't believe this day is here and you guys are going to the prom." At that moment there was a knock at the door and in came Terrance looking sharper than ever. His tuxedo was white, his bow tie was purple on one side and lavender on the other and to top that off he had one shiny purple shoe and one lavender shoe. He opened his jacket and his vest was purple on one side and lavender on the other. Tori and I was so amazed.

"Terrance you really did that coordination good. You really made my day," I said.

"Terrance you are such a doll. You did your thing and made us both happy. We should win for the best attire," said Tori.

We took more pictures and some by the limo. When we arrived at the prom all eyes were on us. Everyone came up to us to take pictures. Even the parents. We went into the prom and the room was so beautiful. We dance together and Terrance gave us both a single dance. We had such a good time. We sat down and talked about the schools we were accepted into. Terrance said that he picked Pennsylvania State and Temple University. I said I was accepted to Penn State with a full scholarship.

"What?" Terrance said, "that's cool Carla."

"I'm not going away to no fancy school. I will be doing community College," said Tori.

"That's good too Tori. At least you be staying in school. Please don't give up on your design. You are too talented to sleep on your gift. Look at all the praise we got on our outfits," I told her.

"Drawing these dresses just got me motivated again." We dance some more. Then they call for the best outfit, and we all won. Tori spoke and told how she designed the dresses. Everyone wanted her number so she could design something for them. We all were dropped off at our houses and I couldn't wait to get inside to tell everyone how my night was.

I told them we had such a great night and how we received a trophy for the best outfit.

"They gave it to me to hold first. Tori received so many numbers from girls wanting her to make them an outfit. Terrance got accepted into Temple University. They have one of the best Dental programs.

"Well Carla," Ms. Blackwell said, "you are the second in your class. Do you know how much of an honor that is baby? Your mother would be so proud of you. You already know that we are."

"I can't wait to see you sissy walk across that stage," said Calvin.

The next day we all went to help Aunt Mimi move her stuff into her new place. It was a nice house and plenty of room for her and the girls. The girls were upset that they were not going to live with their mother right away. Aunt Mimi told them that they will be coming, that she just needs to get everything they need for the house. Then they will be allowed to be with her alone so she can be a good momma to them both. I asked Aunt Mimi was she still coming to my graduation tomorrow. She said she wouldn't miss it for the world.

The next morning was the graduation ceremony. I was so

happy this day was finally here. I was the second person to march down the aisle behind the Valedictorian. I was so nervous because I was the Salutatorian which meant I have to speak and introduce the Valedictorian. This was a great honor. I felt that with all the things that was going on in my life that my grades would have been all over the place. But unbeknownst to me, I managed to keep up my GPA that earned me a full scholarship.

When they announce the awards, I was overjoyed to know that the scholarship was truly mines. I received many awards that day. Terrance received a scholarship as well to Temple University with a full scholarship for his studies as well. Tori got many awards as well with a thousand-dollar grant and a two thousand dollars scholarship to continue her talents in designing. We all were so overwhelmed with what we accomplished in the four years of high school, with all the challenges we had to deal with.

Once we left the graduation ceremony, we went to the restaurant to eat. Then back home where I was giving more gifts from the family. I was happy and crying at the same time because I did it. I truly didn't believe that I would get to this point of my life. It seem like I was in over my head. I thought that I was going to be stuck in the children's home forever. I'm so thankful that God and my momma was watching over me. Now I'm ready for this new chapter in my life. Blessings upon Blessings.

Serina Garland

Two weeks later, I met Terrance and Tori at the mall. We had lunch and talked about a lot of things. We all promised that we will never forget about each other or the CTT Gang. When I got home, Ms. Blackwell handed me a letter. It was address from Riverside Correctional Facility. It was from my dad. I looked at the letter and threw it on the dresser. I was not ready to hear what he had to say. All these years. *"Now you write!"*

I was very upset, angry, and mad. I dropped down at the end of my bed, and just started blasting him out in my journal.

Why? Why Now? Who are you? I'm content and happy. I don't even know what title to give you right now. I felt abandoned. I felt left out, I felt forgotten, I felt that I wasn't worth the fight. I can go on and on. This bullshit just isn't right because you left us! You never tried to figure out how to protect or love us. Momma was counting on you to be there and to care for us. Yet you gave up. You left and we had to endure this mess without you. I had no one. Momma was gone. My father was in prison, and Calvin was in his own messed up world. So, what do you want? I grew up. I figured this mess out all by myself. Standing strong on momma's words and the God she taught me about. I'm stronger and better than I was. I'm an overcomer. I went through many trials! "Yet, I stand."

Now you want me to go down memory lane just because you wrote a few words with your right hand. Words that have been long overdue. Man, I truly forgot about you...

I went into the kitchen where everyone was getting ready for dinner. Ms. Blackwell asked did I open the letter from my dad.

"No ma'am!" Calvin looked at me and smiled.

"Carla! Daddy wrote you a letter?"

"I'm not ready to read it yet."

"Carla that's your daddy. No that's my sperm donor."

"Baby, I'm not trying to interfere in your business but we all make mistakes in life and sometimes we have to forgive those that have hurt us. Just take the time to pray about everything and Let God lead you in the right direction baby," says Ms. Blackwell.

"Carla. dad is just trying to get to know you again so that he can talk about why he did what he did. What he was going through, and how he was feeling."

"Calvin I understand what you're saying but I'm not interested in hearing about dad's problems right now. I have my own decisions to work out right now. I'm very thankful that Ms. Blackwell was here to take us in and open up her home for all of us. I'm so thankful for her and I am thankful that you met Dana."

"Look at all that has happened to Aunt Mimi, the girls, and us. We would be in a whirl wind of shit, still fighting to get out from under all the mess that I cried and prayed every day to get from under."

"Yea! But we made it out. Sis, your prayers were heard."

"Calvin, I get it. I'm truly grateful for what God has done for us all. Me personally I'm not ready to open that door right now. Calvin, he abandoned us in my eyes and I know forgiveness count. I get it. I need time Calvin to process my feelings about a man that left us behind."

"But Carla..." Ms. Blackwell put up her hand and told Calvin to let me heal how I need to heal and one day I will come around. I was so glad she stepped in because I was *SO* done talking about it.

Tori

~THE TAKER~

My name is Victoria Rivera, but everyone calls me Tori for short. Sometimes I want to disappear from all the unpleasant things I have seen. Mainly, the things I have to watch as my Mama go through and juggle her different men around. They don't seem to give a damn about her. But every one of them that she meets she calls them her boo thang.

She used to love sketching and making up her own designs, she even found peace in doing it. She told me that she wants to be a fashion designer one day and she love designing clothes. I feel she need to get back to what makes her happy. Follow her dreams. And not the dreams of men that only wants what's between her legs.

My goal is to finish Central High School. So, I can graduate and get into a good college. My Mama used to be more into what Joseph and I was doing. She would always find the time to laugh and talk with us, when she wasn't occupied with one of her many men. These men seem to be some kind of drug that she's addicted to. She thought she found a winner with my father until he cleaned out her bank account and left us stranded with just our belongings. She never mentioned him or ever said another word about him. "ever". So, I never asked about him. He just became a faint memory to me.

After my dad did that to her, my Mama began to spin out of control. Searching for love in all the wrong men. When she met my little brother dad's. He was nice to us all. He was so excited that mama was pregnant and he was finally getting a son. He asked Mama to name his son Joseph after him. But I never understood what he meant when he said that he *"finally"* got him a boy. I just thought that he was over excited, and he meant to say my first child is a boy. By me being young I just shook my head and smiled at my little brother. When he was born I was about 6 or 7 years old, but I've been through some real situations with mama. I had to grow up fast. Mama never questioned the long trips Joseph took since he was a truck driver. He hung around until Mama found out that he had another family in Jersey. "Oops"! So, he did have other children! And Joseph was not his first child, but he was his first son. That was another addiction she dropped leaving her hurt, angry, confused, and searching for love again.

She picked up another addiction, his name was Victor. When she met Victor "everything changed." Victor was Sophie's dad and he never spent any time with her. He was always in and out of our house like he paid bills here and coming over drunk. So, Sophie just said dada. Just because that's who babies seem to call first. Even though, he never spends any time with Sophie or showed any love or affection to any of us. Mama was ok with just having him around her. She did everything just to please him. He would come over drunk wanting mama to give him money or take him somewhere. His dreams became hers.

He convinced her to put all her savings into his dream of owning a cleaning and laundry. He convinced her the business will be theirs together. Mama went for it, hook line and sinker. So, mama worked hard, and saved more. I found myself having to take care of my siblings more and more every day. It got to the point that mama was always working or doing something with Victor. Sophie started calling me mama because mama wanted to make more money for Victor. She gets so wrapped up, when it comes to these men, that she loses all of her brain cells. While Victor ran around town cheating on her every chance he could. I would see him with other women, but mama was in denial. When she did find out about Victor cheating. Victor would always find a way to convince her that it was all lies. His lies won her over, right into her panties. Once she gave it up to him she'd totally forgot why she was upset with him in the first place.

Mama worked so much these days that we hardly ever seen her. She works for a lawyer's office. They do pay mama real good. She needs to find some time to talk to those attorneys. Maybe they could give her some good advice. However, she always seems to find the time for Victor putting her kids on the back burner again then telling me that this is going to be good for us all which still left me missing and wanting my mother, especially the little ones. I told her that a mother's job is more than just keeping a roof over our head or feeding us. We need her affection and love as well. She would look at me and say, Tori ok. I got this. Those are her favorite words to me now.

When mama gets home, she's always exhausted from work. She would just go straight to her room without a word to us. Now, I'm left taking care of Sophie and Joseph once again. It seems like I could never catch a break on doing anything for myself. My designs were being put on hold for the sake of me playing mama to my brother and sister. I asked her when she would be able to give us any of her time. She would say that Victor wants her to do this for the cleaner's and do that for the laundromat. She said she doesn't have time for this or that which left me asking her, *what do you mean Mama*!

I said with bass in my voice. "Mama we need you too! When would you be able to just be our mother, so I could go back to being a child again?" She looked at me.

"Cállate Tori! This is for us all!" Her Spanish always seems to seep out when she's angry with me but not Victor!

"Yeah but that's what you keep telling me but what is Victor doing?" She gave me a dirty look.

"Just shut up and stop asking me questions!"
I found myself sitting in my own thoughts thinking about how many men Mama had coming in and out of our lives. She never paid attention to who she allowed around us. She never took the

time to sit us down and talk to us or even ask us questions, about the strangers she brought into our home. That's what they were to us, strangers. How can she teach us about strangers' dangers, yet she's the one bringing these strangers to our home? She never told us who they were or where they came from?

A mother should always be aware of the strangers she brings into her home and around her children. You might think you know them, but how well do you. I Thank God every day that they never tried anything with us. I was the one always looking out for us all. Even though, the older I got the wiser I felt I become.

Sylvia never found a real man to love her the way a real man should. She just love them and the lies that came with them. They all told her the same lying ass stories, and she believed them all. She spends most of her time taking care of them and living off every word they say. I don't think that she got the memo that a man is supposed to take care of his woman or you help take care of each other. Sylvia found out many times that they were not who they said they were. They didn't produce to her what they said they would. She always found herself in so many baby mama dramas, or what the hell you're doing with my husband problems. She was always getting caught up in altercation with other women. That it didn't even matter what they said to her. It only matters what the man that she was with at that time said. I couldn't understand why? My mother felt that she needed to have a man on her side. Sylvia allowed these men to fill her head with dreams and lie's. Every time she meets a different man there was always some kind of issue with them! But mama never questioned any of it.

Now!! Here we go again. "Victor"! He's the emotional villain in her life. He is just another compulsive liar who is playing games with her heart, emotions, and mind. But mama is so in love again that she believes everything that Victor tells her.

I often find her in a daze, spaced out with this sad look upon her face. I could see the tears forming in her eyes. I wondered what she be thinking about. What was it that was making her so sad? I asked her what was the matter. She would only say nothing, "Mamacita."

My mother never told the story behind her pain. So, I stopped asking her for now. One day I came home from school and found her crying on the bathroom floor. I didn't know what happen, so I screamed her name.

" Mama what's wrong? Go away!" She would tell me.

"No mama! What's wrong?" Victor didn't want her anymore because she's with child.

"Tori, you don't understand."

"Mama please help me to understand. I think I've been through the struggle with you, so if anybody understand it's me.

Whenever you fall mama, I'm left to pick up the pieces. I'm left to play mama again to my younger sister and brother."

"What did Victor say? What are you going to do?" Mama got up off the floor and went into the living room. Sophie was playing in her playpen. She stops and stares at mama.

"Victor doesn't want any more kids, Tori."

"Why do you want any more from him? He's not even helping you with Sophie."

"I have to do something."

" What are you talking about? Do what Mama?"

"I can't have this baby!" she cried.

"Mama, what are you talking about?" I yelled?

"Victor will come back if I don't have this child."

"What Mama? What are you saying?"

"Tori shush! I got this!" There was nothing else said about that situation. Mama was so out of it for a few days. I was the mama bear fending for my siblings again. Mama didn't even go to work for a couple of days and she is one to never miss a day. Even when she's not feeling well. I came home to find Sophie soaking wet in urine and screaming her head off because she was hungry and needed to be change. She even forgot to pick up Joseph twice.

"Mama, you got to get out of this funk. You got to get it together. Your kids, I repeat *Your* kids need you!"

"Tori, Cállate!"

"Why you keep telling me to shut up, Mama! That's all you say to me now, why? Are you even listening to what I'm saying?" She just left and went in her room again. That's where she goes when she doesn't want to hear the truth. After that. I missed a couple of days out of school. Terrance and Carla called wanting to know if everything was ok. I lied and just said yes, and I'll be there tomorrow. I knocked on my mother's door to let her know I have to go to school before we have more problems.

"Yeah, yeah," she mumbled.

When I came home Friday from picking up Joseph and Sophie, mama was out of her room laying on the couch. She did muster up the nerve to tell me that she was good. That she got it together now.

This weekend she moved around, doing things in the house. She was even on the phone laughing. I hope it wasn't with Victor because this entire time mama was in her depressed mode. I guess that's what it was. We haven't seen no damn Victor. Once Victor got back on speaking terms with mama. He started asking her for money again. She started to see less and less of Victor. Victor always seems to appear when there were other things that need to be brought or done to the building...so he said.

Sylvia never took the time to question him on any of the things he said he needed the money for. She just gave it to him and didn't ask for a receipt. I asked mama could we go see the shop and how it's coming along.

"No Mamacita. Victor got everything under control."

When victor was around, mama was so happy and couldn't keep herself still. She would act so silly giggling at everything he said. Whenever, Victor called her to the room that was the last we would see of her for the night. The next moment you would hear mama moaning and groaning. I would turn the TV up loud enough so that the kids didn't hear the sounds coming from out the room. That left me to attend to the kids once again. Mama played this schoolgirl role, like she was still pondering over a boo thang. I'm getting real fed up with all this "bullshit." She keeps forgetting that she has children and she is a grown ass woman. I tried to tell mama that Victor is not trying to help her.

"He's only taking and taking from you and you keep giving it to him. He's not helping you with this business mama. He's just taking your money and you are paying for everything. He's not doing a damn thing! Did you go see how far the business is going. Or how long are you going to keep believing him. Mama you are killing yourself trying to do all this by yourself. He keeps coming over here telling you he have to get stuff. He's taking from you like you're his own personal ATM."

She tried to convince me that Victor was getting things in place.

"Yes Mama with your money!"

"Tori, you don't understand."

"Well, ayu`dame a entender (help me to understand) Sylvia!" Mama just looked at me and told me to get out of her face. Fine, I said and went to my room and slammed the door.

A few days later mama was in such a better mood that she took the time to play with Joseph and Sophie. It's been a long time since I seen a smile on my mother's face.

"Umm, are you ok, mama?" she told me that she was good and that we are all going out tonight.

"On a Thursday?" Mama was smiling. I was so excited! Until she dropped the bomb and said that Victor was going too. We went to a Spanish restaurant and mama told me to order whatever I wanted.

Victor was all over mama kissing her on her neck playing with Sophie even saying kind words to Joseph and me. That made her feel so special. Once the night was over and it was time to pay the bill, Victor walked away from the table. He went outside to smoke a cigarette. "Night over", "Role playing done", "Back to life", and "Back to reality." So, guess who was left paying the tab and the tip? I looked at mama.

"Tori not tonight, not tonight." We all got into Victor's car and he stopped at the gas station and told mama to go fill it up. Mama didn't even ask Victor where was the money. She just went to get the gas as if her daddy told her to do something. Victor got out of the car and started talking to this lady, it looked like he knew her already for this lady was all over him. I kept watching the door to see if mama was going to come out and catch him touching the lady on her butt. When mama came to the car, she seen Victor grab the lady breast and said something in her ear. Mama yelled, Victor what are haces (you doing)? The lady laughed and got into her car. Victor told mama to Silencio (be quiet) y subir al carro (and get in the car). Mama yelled at Victor all the way home until Victor got tired of telling her to shut up. The next thing you know, he backed handed her right in the mouth.

"What the hell is wrong with you! Don't hit my mother!" Mama told me to be quiet. Once we got home, mama told me to take the kids upstairs and she stayed outside begging Victor to forgive her. I heard her say this as I was walking up the steps. *Forgive you* for WHAT!! Is what I wanted to say. I'm shocked at my mama, but then again, I'm not! I'm not even surprised that she would allow Victor to carry her that way.

Mama came in the house bawling her eyes out, saying that she shouldn't have done that.

"Done what? What did you do?"

"It's my fault that Victor is upset."

"Why Mama! You didn't do nothing wrong."

"Victor left, saying he need time to think."

"Think about what Sylvia? I always call my Mama by her

first name when she makes me mad. I can't believe she's standing right in my face crying like a little child whose father just scolded her.

"Mama!" I yelled. "Sophie is crying the baby needs you."

"Tori you get her I can't right now." She slammed her bedroom door. We did not see her anymore that night. I shook my head at the thought of what just happened. I couldn't believe that after all that, she's blaming herself. I heard her on the phone crying for Victor to come back and forgive her. Victor never came to the house that night. I often wondered why Victor never stayed overnight at the house with mama. They been dealing with each other for over two years. I wondered if she even questioned him on that. This is the cycle I need to break. I wouldn't want a user like Victor.

Mama woke up looking like a mess this morning. You can tell that she was crying all night. She's walking around like a zombie, acting like she can't get it together.

"Mama, Joseph and Sophie need breakfast."

"Tori, take care of them."

I never told my mother no nor talked back to her before, but I felt she needed a reality check.

"Mama, I have to go to school. You're the mother so act like it!"

"Tori be quiet! Don't you talk to me that way."

"Well Mama! I can't keep being their mother. You're their Mama. They need you! Get Victor out your head and take care of things."

Sylvia keeps letting Victor take away all her positive energy and that's why her own family choose not to come around. They got tired of mama letting these different men use her. Now here's Victor and they see that Sylvia hang on to everything he says. My uncle's tried to talk to her but she said to them that it's her life and she got it. So they left her to her life. The only time he stay's over is when he wants something from mama and it's never for more than 24 hours. He knows when to hang onto mama's tits to get what he wants. I've tried to keep my mother from going over the deep end but if she stays with Victor any longer she will lose her mind. Sylvia just doesn't realize how much we need her. She doesn't seem to understand that I am still a teenager and I needs my Mama. I can't be responsible to do her job.

Whenever Sylvia found time to be a Mama to her own kids, I would take that time to go to the library to collect my thoughts and read up on all my favorite clothing designers. My favor designer is Stella McCartney and I just love her designs.

That was the day that I met Terrance. Terrance was sitting at the same table looking clueless. I asked him was he ok. Terrance looked up, stared at me, and asked me if I was talking to him? I smiled and said yes. I've seen many of those blank stares before. Immediately he felt a sense of concern in my eyes and he found himself talking to me about his pain. I listened attentively because I understood how he was feeling.

Terrance was going on and on about his Mama which made him get upset that he started to get louder and angry, with frustration. The librarian lady told us to be quiet or leave. So, we ended the conversation and exchange numbers. Terrance said I was a good listener and we became good friends from that day on. I was still disappointed in my Mama. She's always letting Victor walk all over her.

When I got home, Victor was there and mama was all smiles. I looked at Victor and shook my head.

"Hey Tori baby," goes mama. "Mama going to need you tonight."

"For what Mama?"

"To take care of your brother and sister. Victor and I are going to have date night."

"Mama, Vamos! (Come on). Victor looked at me with a wicked stare.

"Girl! Did you hear what your mother said? She's not asking you she is telling you!"

I looked at my mother to see if she was going to correct him. She didn't of course. I looked at Victor.

"Man please. Tune eres mi papa!" (you're not my dad)

Mama yelled, Tori, Silencio (be quiet)!! Victor looked at mama.

"See, this the shit I don't have time for!" he shouted out loud. Of course, I just clammed up and said whatever Mama.

When mama left with Victor, I got Sophie down and Joseph curled up on the couch beside me and we cuddled together and watched TV.

"Tori, what's wrong with Mama?" Joseph said with a look of sadness on his innocent face.

"What do you mean Joseph?"

"Why do Mama let Victor be so mean to her?"

"Joseph, I don't know. Mama thinks she's in Love. But Love is not supposed to hurt. I want you to always remember that a man is supposed to treat a woman, or his wife with love and respect. When you get older, always remember to respect, and treat your girlfriend or wife with the upmost respect and honor her because women are precious jewels.

"Tori, I promise I will," he said.

It was getting late and I was tired of waiting up for Mama. The phone rang and she was on the other end.

"Tori baby, mama going to spend the night out with Victor." Victor could be heard in the background yelling for her to get off the phone.

"Tori, I have to go." That was the weekend that Mama

didn't come back until Sunday night. She was all smiles. When she got home, she started talking about her weekend.

"The weekend was nice. We talked about the business. It's all coming together good Tori. I had a wonderful time with Victor. He makes me so happy."

"But Mama, Victor knows that you have children and Sophie is his. Why does he keep taking you away from your children? You are a mother and I am only 15 years old. You are still responsible for me as well as my brother, and sister. You are supposed to be here with your children. Watching over us and keeping us safe at night, but you're out gallivanting around with Victor. It doesn't seem that he cares anything about Sophie or your other children for that matter. Mama I just want to know where does your responsibility lies?"

"Tori be quiet! Don't you dare talk to me like that!"

"Mama, I'm sorry but this is too much for me. I need you Mama."

"I'm right here baby. Everything is going to be alright, Mamacita."

"Mama, I got friends coming over next weekend is it ok?"

"Tori, that's fine. Victor said he was taking me out again next weekend."

I was happy that I was having company over, especially since this will be the first.

Serina Garland

Terrance, Carla, and her twin cousins all arrived around the same time. Joseph was so happy to have other kids to play with. He didn't mind that they were girls. Sophie was being extra good today. I wonder if she knew that this was different for us all. We were all glad that we could see each other outside of school. We talked about our events at home and how scared we were for each other. We searched the computer to find Terrance's dad first. His dad's name was easy to find. We searched Facebook first. Terrance Oliver Mitchell. There was a couple of names so we went through them all. There was about 20 Terrance Oliver Mitchell. We went through them by States first. We eliminated the ones by their ages, and races. Which left us with 9. So, we started going through their pages but none of them fitted the profile. We took a break to feed the kids some lunch.

"Tori, the girls are really having a good time. They don't get out much. Just to go to school or when I take them to the park. They needed to get out of that house. Carla told me everything that has happened.

"Did you tell Calvin yet?"

"No because I feared what Calvin would do."

"Carla," Terrance goes, "you must tell somebody. What if he tries that again? Or hurt the girls when you not there?"

"I know! I have to figure this out. You just don't know what we have to deal with in that house. Some of it is too embarrassing to repeat. I know that the girls need me there. I often wonder what they've been through before I got there. Aunt Mimi is always spaced out somewhere." Carla shook the thought away because it was upsetting her.

"What about you Terrance? Are you going to tell your mother what you heard?"

"I'm going to try. The thing is will she listen and believe me. I just feel that something is not right about him. I just can't put my finger on it yet. I just want her to be aware and see that this man is not for her at all."

"That's what I'm trying to tell my Mama. She is so in love with this man or the thought of her just having one, that she doesn't see that he's not even treating her with respect. He doesn't even spend any quality time with Sophie and she's his own daughter. She doesn't even know him as daddy. She just says dada because Mama drills it in her. Did I tell you guys that my mother is supposed to be having a baby?'

"What!" We both said.

"That's what she's been crying about a couple of days ago. She said that Victor didn't want any more kids. So, I don't know. She's happy now and haven't said another word about it."

"Tori, where is your Mama, now?" Carla asked.

"Oh girl! She went out last night. On a date with Victor or that's what she's calling it. She really thinks she's a schoolgirl. She called me to say that she was staying out again. I told her about leaving us in the house at night by ourselves, but I guess she don't care because she did it again. She doesn't even care that Victor is keeping her from her children." No sooner then I said that the door opens and in pops my mother with a bloody nose and a black eye. Tori jumps up and ran to her mother to ask what happen?

"Are you ok?" Sylvia seen all of us and was instantly embarrassed doing a beeline straight to her room.

She called Tori to come here in Spanish. At that time Terrance and I was already gathering up our things to leave. The girls didn't want to go but it was time. When Tori came back in the living room, she was flush because she didn't want to tell us that we had to leave. So, I broke the ice for her and said girl I must get these girls back before their mother have a fit. Terrance said Tori I have to go too. I really enjoyed my day with you guys.

I went into the room to see if my mama was ok. I asked her what happened? She said she was having a good time with Victor and when we were at a restaurant eating, this woman came up to the table.

"Tori, she was pregnant and was yelling at both Victor and me. She wanted to know who I was? I asked her what business is that of yours, she said bitch this is my man. I told her he's been my man for two years now. Victor looked at me and told me to shut the fuck up. She started hitting Victor and calling him a cheater. I asked Victor what is she talking about? And he told me to be quiet. The woman said, did this fucking cheater tell you that we were having another baby and I'm eight months pregnant? I looked at Victor. Another baby! I yelled at him and he pushed me in the chair and told me to sit down and don't say a damn word!"

"What Mama?!"

"Tori I was in shock. I sat there like a fool trying to calm myself down. I had all kinds of thoughts going through my head I thought this was my man but the joke was on me because he was apparently somebody else's man. I felt like I was being punked. I realized that he was taking a long time to get back to me. I went outside and he was hugged up with this woman. Trying to explain himself to her. I asked him what was going on and he said shut up bitch and hauled off and slapped me in the damn face, Tori!"

"Mama! What?"

"I yelled at him what the hell are you doing? Victor we have a child together and then he punched me in the nose. He had the nerve to say to this woman, that my child was in question. I yelled *that child*! Our daughter's name is Sophie. I said. Right there I woke the fuck up. Her name was Marisol and she told Victor to get off of her and take his ass with me. He said no I don't want her. I said I don't want your lying, cheating ass either. He told her that he wanted her. I looked at Victor in disbelief. I couldn't even say anything. I was so humiliated with so much pain. I was looking him straight in the face and I realized that I never knew this man. I just fell in love at the thought of having one Tori. I never took the time to check him out. I told myself that I would, before I get into another relationship this time. I should've! This bastard pushed me out the way, to help her in the car. Yes Mamacita. He Left me standing there bleeding and crying. I walked away and waved a cab down. I was hurting so much inside. I couldn't believe what this man just did to me. I cried my eyes out because he told me he didn't want any more kids. So, I had an abortion Tori!"

"Mama! Why? Why you do that?"

"Tori he didn't want it. He said he couldn't afford it. That bastard told me that he didn't want any more kids and all along she's eight months pregnant and have other kids with this bastard. Tori! What the hell? He slapped me and punched me in the nose to prove a point to this woman. All that I give him. All that I allowed him to take from me. He comes over here asking me for money like he had it like that. Asking me for this and that. Like a fool I give it to him. I feel so stupid right now. He really used me and played with my emotions. He never gave me any of it back baby. Always said he would. All the money he came and got he said it was for the business. I never asked him for one receipt or even took time to go look at the place to see the things he said we needed. I kept my mouth shut like a scared little bitch.

I was afraid that I was going to lose him. "Not anymore"! It's my turn. I'm going to show him better than I can tell him!"

Mama started crying more every time she thought about what Victor did. He woke her up! At least her feelings because I never seen that side of Sylvia before. Well, it's about damn time. I said to myself. She went into her room where she continued to cry for hours. Sylvia did mope around the house, but she mustered up enough strength to go to work. This went on for about two weeks. She didn't answer any of his phone calls. He came to the house, but she did not let him in. He even had the nerve to come by drunk saying that he wanted to see his child. Sylvia yelled at him saying you don't have a child here remember, *she's in question*. That really set mama off. She told him to get from in front of her door before she calls his baby mama.

I found mama holding Sophie more and playing with the kids a lot. She said that she's feeling great.

"I feel so ashamed how I allowed myself to let this stupid ass man clog my judgment. Victoria this shit just woke me the hell up and I'm going to work hard to give us something better." I didn't know what she was talking about, but things sure was different about her because she called me Victoria.

The next morning, she was in the kitchen making breakfast for us and listening to her music.

"How you feeling, mama?"

"Ok? Tori I'm good. You can relax baby. I got this."

Mama always says that and for some reason I believed her this time. Victor kept calling mama and she kept hanging up. This went on for about 3 weeks. She kept going to work. Still staying late and I was still left taking care of Joseph and Sophie. I haven't had a chance to talk to Terrance and Carla. Every day I had to go straight to Joseph school, then pick up Sophie from the babysitter. Even though Victor wasn't around. Mama was working more. She claimed she have to get this business off the ground.

When we got home, mama was sitting at the table with Victor. I gave my mother a puzzled look.

"What's up, mama?" Looking from her to Victor then back to her.

"Nothing Tori. Take the kids in the room."

"Hey baby come to daddy," Victor said to Sophie but Mama stepped in.

"No! Tori, please take her in the room." I could hear mama yelling at Victor.

"She said no you're not going to do that. You said she's in question, remember"

"Sylvia, what are you talking about? I was just trying to keep the peace."

"BY HITTING ME!" That's cool Victor let's just leave it up to

DANA to decide! So, you can have the real proof. You will never tell anyone else that *she's in question.*"

"Come on Sylvia, let's not go there." He begged.

"No, you took me there. Victor I forgot to get the receipts for the materials you got for the shop. I went down there and there's not one thing that I can see that you brought. Where is the money, better yet the receipts? I just need you to sign these papers and produce the materials for the business."

Victor looked dumbfounded. "Huh, why are you asking about receipts for?"

"Victor I need to get these papers signed so the contractor can start working on the shop." Mama knew Victor wasn't going to read the papers. All he wanted was to hear that she was still working on getting the business together. He didn't realize that he was signing papers to take his name off of all the businesses. Little did he know, the shops now solely belong to Sylvia Rivera.

"The shop is almost ready to open," he goes.

"Well, I need you to show me the receipts of all the merchandise you brought with the money I gave you because I haven't seen anything yet."

Victor told mama that he got the supplies and the receipts at the house.

"Why are they at the house? They should be in the shop. I

just need more money to pay the contractor to put in the machines. I'll take care of that."

"No!" Victor shouted. "That's my job. Well, you don't seem to be showing me any progress and I haven't seen anything new that *I* paid for.

Victor yelled at mama and said *we*. Mama just looked at him.

"It's time for you to leave." Victor stood up and grabbed her and she pushed him off of her. Victor looked at her.

"What's up baby?" Mama looked at Victor and roll her eyes up in her head.

"It's not that type of party anymore Victor. This is about our business." Sylvia called me to come in the living room. Like she wanted me to do something, but I know it was just so she could get him to leave.

Mama really is not feeling Victor anymore. I could see that through her demeanor. Victor walked over to her.

"What do you want?" Victor looked at her sideways.

"Woman, you need to stop this shit. We need to get this business together." Sylvia looked at Victor with a sly grin.

"That's what we are doing? You the one who need to stop asking me for money for stuff and not buying it. Let me ask you again Victor. What have you been doing with all the money that I've been giving you for supplies?"

"I did get them."

"Ok, so where they at? I'm doing my job woman. Stop coming for me." Sylvia shook her head and looked at him.

"Whatever! Leave!" she screamed at him. I am so proud that my mother is standing her grounds. Victor really hit a core that *woke her up*. I think it's the pain in her heart that bothers her the most. Especially when you tell a woman that their child is in question. I really did see a change in Mama. She spends more time with the kids when she is not working late. She talks to us more, make us meals like a Mama should. I'm so sorry that Mama had to go through that abuse with Victor. Before, she realized that she didn't need him. I think that she is over men taking her for granted. Mama was at a point where she was tired of thinking that a man can do for her what she can do for herself. Sometimes we are so caught up in our own stuff that we lose the sight of the ones that we supposed to be caring for. I know that mama loves us and I know that she needs someone in her life but my mother has a good head on her shoulders and she's a very talented woman and I think that she can be and do all that she needs to do without Victor or any man. Weeks and days went by and Mama was up late burning the midnight oil. It seem that Mama had so much time on her hands now, that she doesn't spend all of her time worrying about Victor. I see Mama scheduling things like she used to before. I can see a difference in her. Mama was good at designing stuff. She used to draw a lot of beautiful things and beautiful sceneries.

I really do love designing clothing too, but since I've been taking care of Joseph and Sophie I haven't had time to get back into my designs for myself. I miss my friends and I can't even spend any time with them. I spend most of my days playing mama. I don't even get to talk to them or know what's been going on in their lives. I can't hardly remember anything about my junior year. We all were so busy making sure we do what we had to at home that we didn't have any time to meet each other at the bleachers anymore. I miss those days. It allowed us to open up and tell each other of our struggles. I was upset that they were going through sad times as well. I just was relieved that I had friends that took the time to listen to me and I can help them feel at ease with their family struggles as well. I understand that many people have problems where they need to vent to one another about. We all have our own battles to fight and we are doing everything to stay on top.

The next thing I knew, I was a Senior. I know it's time for me to choose some colleges. I really was not excited about doing that either. I'm not in a hurry, because I don't want to go to college right away. I still think I need to be around for my siblings. I got so wrapped up being their big sister and helping them with what I could that I'm just not ready to leave at this time.

Terrance called me out of the blue and said that he wanted to talk to Carla and me at the same time so we did a three way on the phone. We were shocked at what Terrance told us about his Mama and about him going to jail. He said that he had to let us know since we were his best friends. He asked could we come to the funeral. Of course, we both said yes. When I got off the phone I told Mama what had happened and that I need to be there for him. She understood and said (Toros tienes que ir).Tori you must go.

Carla and I went to the funeral together. I ended up reading the poem Carla wrote for Terrance's mother funeral because Carla's nerves was off the chain. It just brought back too many memories of her Mama. We didn't go to the burial but we did go to the house to be there when Terrance got back. We stayed for a long time talking and catching up. Finding out what we all had been through.

Sylvia was busy all the time now working to get the business up and going. Although, I'm still watching after my siblings, Sylvia was at the table sketching designs and making signs for the shop. I try not to complain a lot because I'm happy to see my mother's passion for what she loves doing. Seeing her passion was what got me interested in designing in the first place. Having my Mama home more and interacting with us all was a blessing. I prayed for this. Not seeing Victor was an extra blessing. Even Joseph was happy that he was not always over as he now gets time to spend with his mother. I'm so glad that the kids got their mother back, for I don't know if this was developing any scars in their little minds.

Mama took me with her to see the shop. I was so impressed at how far the business was coming together.

"Mama, I'm really proud of what you have accomplished."

"Tori, I brought you here to see how far I had come in getting this business off the ground. I need you to know that I took out a loan to front this place and Victor name is not on it. This will be a shock to him on opening day," she said happily.

I looked at her, waiting for her to continue telling me what she wanted me to know.

"Tori, it was like something in my mind shifted when Victor did what he did. I don't know why this incident was the one that woke me up. But I'm glad that I'm back. Victor truly was not the one for me. I'm sorry that I had an abortion, but God knows I didn't need to be trapped with this man and his issues. I know that I was giving this man my money and he was taking care of the next bitch with it. So, I want you to know that this is my business and mine's alone. Victor hand is not in this. My lawyer did all the paperwork so I own this business. By myself. I want to keep it a secret from Victor."

"Mama, well you know that I'm not saying anything to him." So, she continues with letting me know that she took out a loan to get everything started. Sylvia wanted to change the direction of her life. To make up for all the bad decisions that she made. Not being a responsible adult to her children. Giving all of her attention to Victor. She was so wrapped up in being in love with him that she allowed him to take her away from her kids, take money out of her kids' mouths, and taking away her respect for herself. She shook her head in disbelief in knowing how vulnerable and naïve she was in giving into the words that these men would tell her. She couldn't believe how she dodge the bullet from only having three children, if she wasn't so in love with Victor she would have had baby number four. She was so happy that he convinced her that he didn't want another child. The pain sunk in when she found out that he was having a child with another woman. Now, she knows why he was so adamant about her getting an abortion. Sylvia played that day back in her head. She was mad, used, but glad that she was not going to be control by anyone who didn't care about her or her children. Now it was Sylvia's turn to show Victor that he underestimated her and her working at a lawyer's office really did pay off for her. *I'll show him that I do have a brain and my own goals.*

My Mama was up again sketching and making up more signs for the business. I looked at the design and told her that they were nice.

"I'm glad that you like them. Can you design a sign to put

over the store?" She changed the name of her business.

"Victor's name will not be on this building. I began sketching the design. I brought the supplies and I took out the loan. I hired the construction workers. So, I'm calling it *Sylvia's Laundry/Clean up Service*. Do you think you can design something wonderful to set the business off?" I was all smiles. I couldn't believe that my Mama was giving me a big job like this.

"Yes Mama!" I happily replied, "I'm going to do a great job. Are you sure though? You want me to do it and not a professional sign maker?"

"I would get it professionally made, but only with the designs you make." I was happy that she gave me this honor. This will help surely motivate me in getting back into my designs again.

"Mama Terrance asked me to the prom and he asked Carla too. So, I'm designing our dresses as well. Carla wants her dress to be purple. I want lavender. I'm so excited that Terrance asked us both to the prom. And when I graduate, I don't want to go to college right away."

"I want you to go to college to continue learning all that you need to know about designing."

"I will, Mama. I'm not going to stop designing because it's my dream to see other people wearing my design. I just want to take a year off Mama."

"Tori, maybe you can work in the cleaners some days to put a little money in your pocket. I also called your Tio and Tia to come and help me with the business." I looked at my Mama in amazement. She is really learning how to put things behind her and build a relationship with her family again. Thank God Victor is out of this picture.

Once I got home, Victor was knocking on our door.

"Where's your Mama?"

"How would I know? I just got here." I knew my Mama was home because she got off early to pick up Sophie ad Joseph. I went to unlock the door and Victor tried to push his way in.

"You can't come in here. My Mama isn't home!"

"Move girl! I can come in and wait for her!"

"Oh, that's definitely not gonna happen!" I slammed the door in his face. When I looked down the hall I seen Mama coming out of the room with her finger on her lip telling me to be quiet. I looked out the peephole and Victor was gone.

"Mama, what happen? Why didn't you answer the door?"

"I'm not ready to go back in forth with Victor just yet."

"What's going on?"

"He probably tried to get into the shop and realize his keys didn't work. I changed the locks on his ass. He's not giving me anything towards the opening of that place. He just keeps coming here thinking that everything is still the same. I get it now

Mamacita. Victor was just using me to fund this business for him. Then he was going to run that shit with that hoe. He's not dealing with a weak woman anymore. I won't let him take my money and my hard work off my family table ever again. He's really in for a rude awakening when the revealing of the shop comes up." Sylvia laughed. I got to see a lot more of my Tia and Tio's. Sylvia was showing them the layout of the business and what their job would be.

My Mama was really on top of her game. She was so determined to get everything in order for the opening day. The next day Carla and I met up, so that we can get fitted for our dresses. I designed both of our dresses and they fit us perfectly. We both look stunning in them. We couldn't wait for the day to wear them to the prom. Carla got a chance to tell me a little about what was going on in her life. I told her a little about what was going on in mine. I don't always tell them everything that I'm going through. I know that I should because it always helps to talk your situation out with those you love and are close with. Sometimes talking to a psychiatrist can help smooth things out in your head as well. So, people won't feel stuck and depressed with things that they cannot change for themselves. I always felt that Carla and Terrance struggles were much more serious than what I was going through right now.

"Tori, I know that things are not as they should be for us

all, but I know that better days are coming. It's our turn to put some smiles on our faces. The prom is approaching us all and we should all have our day. Remember what we said about the CTT group. That we will not burden ourselves down with things that we cannot change, but we will try our best to achieve doing everything we can to not repeat the cycle," Carla exclaimed.

I was so overwhelmed with tears in hearing my friend say those words, because it let me know that no matter what problems she's dealing with, she found the time to let me know that this too shall pass.

No sooner than I got in the house. Victor came banging on the door...again! This time mama answered.

"What do he want?"

"What do you mean, what do I want? Woman, we need to talk about the shop and you need to give me some money, so that I can buy the things for the business. Sylvia you need to open the door," Victor demanded.

"I don't have anything to say to you and I'm not going to give you any more money. You thought I was stupid. You did not buy any supplies or pay the contractor like you said."

"Sylvia? Baby? What are you talking about? Why my keys not opening up the shop?"

"Victor, leave from in front of my door. We will talk about this another time."

"No! Hell no!" He yelled out. "I want to talk about it now! I also want to see my daughter. Not today Victor, not today."

"What are you talking about woman? You can't keep me from my daughter?"

"Watch me! Victor, just go to your baby mama. She didn't have your child yet?" Victor started banging on the door again insisting that mama open it up and let him in.

"No Victor! I'm not doing this shit with you. And I'll call the cops to have them remove you from in front of my door!" Victor quickly vacated the premises.

"Mama, what are you going to do about this man? He's going to keep coming around bothering you. Mama said Tori, don't you worry about this. Remember I work for a lawyer's office and they will handle him for me." Sylvia then got on the phone and was talking to one of my uncles about what just happened.

She talked to one of the lawyers at her office and after talking to Mr. Allen, he advised her of what to do.

Sylvia went to the courthouse the next morning to get custody papers for Sophie, so that Victor wouldn't try doing anything stupid. Sylvia already had all the documents that shows that she is the sole owner of the business. My mama was not so fascinated or in love with Victor as much as she thought she was. She got those wheels spinning up there now. Was this in her all this time or did it take Victor beating her ass and embarrassing her to the point that her eyes are wide open now and not her nose.

Sylvia is making sure she puts all her ducks in a row. She will not allow Victor to ever think that he would take this business from up under her. She thanks him, for giving her the push. She even thanks him for his mess ups because all the things that she went through with him he knows now that if she didn't put an end to him taking from her or her giving to him, that he would've just kept on using her.

Mama was on her knees thanking God for removing the scales from her eyes before it was too late. She knew that Victor would leave her assed out. He would try to run the business without her. With all the money and the loan she received, it helped her to establish the business. Sylvia was crying so hard. I came out to see if she was ok.

"I'm so thankful for (Salmos 124:2) Psalms 124:2 (Si no hubiera Sidon por el senor de mi parte). If it had not been for the Lord on my side where would I be.

Sylvia went to the shop to show my Tio and Tia what they would me doing. She knew that my uncle Frank was good at fixing things so the laundromat would be right up his alley. She knew that Marilyn would be good at customer service.

Victor came into the business yelling at Sylvia about her leaving him out of the plans of their place.

"This place is almost ready to be open. I don't have time to argue with you, Victor!"

"What the hell are you talking about?" At that time, both my uncles came from the back which shocked Victor.

"What's going on? I know you was not just yelling at my sister?" Uncle Frank played it off because mama told them all what she's been going through with him. She told them the changes she got her lawyer friend to do and how the business is in her name only. Uncle Frank continued telling mama that all the machines were working well.

"That's good to know since I will be here working as we go forward. I need to know that everything is in good working condition," Victor said.

"Correction Victor, Frank is going to be here attending to the laundromat."

Victor looked at Sylvia with a death stare.

"Oh yeah? We haven't discussed who we were hiring yet baby. I have a couple of people I promise this job to."

Sylvia chuckled. "Well, Victor you never discuss any of that with me. I'm part owner too, right?"

"Ok but they can help get our place up and running."

"Well, I took the liberty of doing that. I already hired some people as well. I also took care of installing all the equipment the business needed." Victor was heated but he would not go back and forth with Sylvia because both my uncles were there.

"Sylvia, I need you to come outside so I can talk to you!" Victor yelled.

"How the hell you going to just change plans on me woman? Who the hell gave you the right to change things without my permission!"

"Oh! So, I need your permission now to make changes on my I mean our business when you're never around for me to talk to you?"

"How are you going to hire your friends to work in this business?" said Sylvia. He thinks that I'm stupid.

"How are you going to make plans without me?" Victor shouted out! "You need to fix this shit and tell your family that we already got people hired for the position."

"Oh, I won't do that Victor! This place is up and ready to go and the grand opening is about a month away."

"You better just figure out what the hell you're gonna do! 'Cause I'm not paying both people. The ones you hired and the ones I hired. Who's paying all of them?"

Sylvia laughed and wanted to tell him to go to hell, but she knew that she had to hold on a little longer.

"So, Victor I'll see what I could do."

Victor yelled, "No you do it and you better before the opening!" Mama smirked then went back inside.

"What are you going to do about Victor when he sees the name of the business changed and his name is not on it?"

Mama said he will find out what the real deal is on the grand opening day. He thinks that everything is still the same. He thinks that he can abuse me and I'm going to allow him to do it again. I was so in love with the thought of having a man. I truly lost who the hell I was. I want him to know that he woke me all the way up. I can't wait to see his face when he sees that name of the business does not say Victor. Victor thinks that I'm so afraid of how things went that day. He thinks that as stupid as I may have acted about all the past things I let him do to me, So I'm going to carry it like he got the upper hand, but I'm going to have the last laugh on his ass on the Grand Opening day.

Mama and my family were all at the house when I was getting dressed for the prom. My uncles couldn't stop snapping pictures of me or telling me how beautiful I was. My uncle drove me to Carla's house, where we all had plan to meet up. We had such a good time at the prom. People that we didn't even know was taking pictures of our outfits. We were the talk of the prom that night. We even won for best coordinating outfits. Once the kid's found out that I made Carla and my dress they started asking me for my phone number, or gave me theirs, so that I could make them an outfit. We all had such a wonderful time at our prom.

This was the best day of our four years in high school. This will be a day that we all will remember. I will miss my friends when they go away to college. We all promised that we will keep in close touch with each other because the CTT group will never slip up. Terrance had said even if we all get married and have children. We all laughed and hugged each other.

Graduation day was coming up and mama was more nervous than me. She grabbed and gave me a big hug.

"I can't believe you're graduating. I'm so proud that you made it through all of my bullshit and crazy moments. I'm very proud of you." She apologized for not being a good mother.

"Although things got out of hand from time to time, you were still my Mama and we still had a roof over our heads and food on the table. I'm just glad that you got it together and that Victor is out of the picture. He really was not good for you at all. He's not even a good dad to Sophie. He was always taking from you Mama. Whether it was your money or your time away from us. The only good thing that came from you being with him verses all the other cats is that you found the strength to draw the line with him. I am so proud that we got our Mama back and you're getting ready to open up your own business. You did this by yourself. Without a man mama. You did it! I'm glad that you are back into doing what you love."

"Tori, I keep forgetting to let you know how much I love the sign you designed. You are good at what you do. Please continue studying all you need to. I see you going far baby girl. I mean it. You are really good."

"I can't wait for opening day too, Mama."

It was finally the grand opening day…May 27 and I graduate on June 7. My Mama, aunt and uncles were very busy getting things in order. Through this whole process, Victor never came around. He knew that since he couldn't get any more money from mama, that there was no need to show his face.

He called Sylvia Monday to see if the business was still going to open up on time.

"Victor, where have you been? You never came around to see if I needed anything for the shop. You told me you got this. So I left you alone. So, you're calling now to see when *we* are going to open?"

"Yes because we still have a business to get up and running. Did you take care of that last thing we were talking about?"

"Yeah, yeah I did."

"Good," Victor said, 'cause I want Marisol to run the cleaners."

"What! Victor there is only one Marisol I know and I know you not trying to squeeze her in to this business."

"Sylvia, that's the mother of my kids. What the hell! Do you want me to do? I have to feed my kids."

"That's not my damn problem, now is it Victor? How dare you think that you can call me with this dumb shit like this and think I'm just supposed to agree with you on this. Victor you better figure out what you're going to tell Marisol or she's gonna be very disappointed."

Sylvia didn't care what came out of her mouth at that point.

"She's going to be very disappointed like you."

"What!" Victor shouted into the phone. "What did you say woman? Woman I can hire anybody I want to work in my shop!"

"Hold up Victor. This is not your shop. This is supposed to be our shop, but I'm gonna let you have that one. Opening day is in four more days. I will see you on that day."

"Wait, Victor said, "I need the key to see how everything is coming together."

"Yeah, yeah, whatever!" Sylvia then hung up. She knew that Victor would never get those keys. She knew she had four more days to give him the run around. Sylvia said to herself, Marisol? Oh, hell to the no. They both got me all fucked up!"

All of my family went to my uncle Paul's restaurant to celebrate my Mama's new business and my graduation. We had such a tremendous time with one another. It was so good to see them all in one place enjoying themselves. Even though they all were not speaking to my Mama, they came together when she really needed them.

Victor happens to call mama wanting to get the keys.

"I'm not at home." Victor heard the noise in the background.

"Where you at?"

"I'm out with my family, why?"

"I need you to stop what you're doing and bring me the damn keys!" Mama started yelling at Victor.

"I can't bring them right now because I've been drinking." Victor got aggressive. "Who are you talking to like that woman! Tell me where you're at so that I can come get them!" Uncle Frank grabbed the phone from mama.

"What's the problem?" He began telling Tio that he wanted the keys to the shop to see the finished work. Tio told him that he would have to wait for another day because my sister is not in any condition to drive or deal with anything tonight."

"Whatever!" Victor said then hung up. Uncle Frank told mama that he was staying at the house for the next two days until the shop is open.

"You can't keep dealing with this man. I don't understand why he thinks that this is his business when he hasn't put a brown penny in the construction, painting, or any other materials. Not one finger in the arrangement, clean up, or the paperwork. Let him come on that day with any mess. I swear all my boys will be there too. He can act like a fool if he wants. He's messing with the wrong sister. I promise you that, sis."

The next day Victor came to the house thinking that Sylvia was there. Uncle Frank opened the door. Victor didn't even know who was opening it. He just started yelling.

"Where's the damn keys at woman?" Uncle Frank looked at him.

"What! Who are you talking to like that?" Victor jumped when he heard a different voice.

"Naw man. I just came to get the keys. Your sister is having me go all out of my way just to get these damn keys."

"Well, as you can see man, she's not here and I better not hear of you talking to my sister like that again. She didn't tell me about no keys. So, to put you at ease man, the place looks very nice from what I've seen. I highly suggest you can stop harassing her now and just wait like the rest of us on opening day. It's tomorrow man and we'll all see it then." Victor left but not before saying a few words.

"That's cool. Just tell Sylvia I came bye."

I asked Terrance and Carla if they would come by to help celebrate my Mama's new shop. They said they would. The next day we all were so busy running around making sure we had everything for the grand opening. The phone just kept ringing and ringing all the time. We all got to the shop around 11:30am for the revealing and cutting was at 12noon. It was so crowded around the shop. There were people everywhere. The crowd was getting bigger and bigger by the minute.

All of my mama friends from her job were there. Mr. Allen was talking to mama and having her sign a few more papers. Victor showed up with the lady and his new baby and the rest of her mob. He went into the shop, looking around like he did some things in there. He came over to mama.

"That's why I wanted to see the place before today. I wanted the machine to go on that side of the room."

"Victor! That's neither here nor there, right now."

Everyone was enjoying the sign and the deals that the business had to offer. Mr. Allen got on the bullhorn to let everyone know that it was time for the ribbon cutting ceremony and the revealing of the name of the business. Victor was acting like he was the big man of the day. He came over to where mama was at as she was getting ready to cut the ribbon. He took the scissors from out of mama's hands.

"I will cut it."

"No, you will not!" Mr. Allen said taking the scissors from Victor.

"Sylvia will be doing the cutting." Victor looked at Mr. Allen.

"This is my business too."

"Hold on Mr. Torres," Mr. Allen said. "I have some papers for you to read and sign. We've been dealing with Ms. Rivera all this time, so she will cut the ribbon." Mama happily cut the ribbon to officially open up the business. My uncle's pulled the string to bring down the drapes to reveal the name of the business. The shop was called *Sylvia's Laundry & Clean Up Service.*

When Victor seen the name, he flipped out.

"What is this shit! Where is my name? Sylvia this is not your shop alone."

Mama looked over to Victor.

"Well Vic, I hate to tell you this but it is. It is all mine alone! You haven't done anything, or gave anything, to help bring this business to life."

Marisol looked to Victor. "What the hell is going on?" All the people he brought with him was yelling at him.

"What kind of shit is this, Vic man? You told us this was your shop. Mr. Allen gave Victor a lot of papers to read. He seen his signature on them.

"I don't remember signing no shit like this!" Victor looked at Sylvia and asked her what the hell did she do.

"This is my business Victor. I put in all the money to get this up and going. I took out the loans. I even brought stuff with my own money." Victor looked at the paperwork he was holding and saw that Sylvia was the owner of the laundry/cleaners. He also got papers showing that Sylvia has sole full custody of Sophie.

Victor was so upset he launched at mama, but my uncles

and their friends were all over him.

"You sorry mother fucker. You thought that I was just going to let you deny my child, punch me in my face for this bitch, leave me bleeding all over the place, and had me stranded and we were still supposed to have a business together. And you want this trash to work here? How weak minded did you think I was, huh? You really thought that I was going to be ok working in the same place with the hoe you had a baby with? No, I mean kids with? Victor, you got me all the way fucked up. Telling me that you didn't want any more children. All the time this hoe was pregnant again with your kid. What number is this? Then you talked me into having an abortion? That was the best thing you ever did for me. Sophie, you remember our daughter whether you deny her or not. That little girl right there, will be just fine." Mama walked away leaving Victor standing there looking stupid. Marisol told Victor that he was such a liar.

"All this time you had me believing that this was your business alone. Just for me to get up here and find out you don't own shit. Living in my house taking my money like you was getting things together for our family. Man, stay away from me and the kids. I can do this shit without you. I don't need you in my life."

"Wait, let me talk to you baby." She got in somebody's car and left him standing there. Sylvia smiled because she just witnessed a deja'vu moment.

People was packing inside the laundromat washing their clothes and taking advantage of the Grand Opening promotions already. Uncle Frank told mama that everything went good today in spite of what Victor thought he was gonna change.

"You have a good business here sis. You're in a good location and this shop will make a good profit for yourself." I was learning a lot about the cleaners from my Tia. I really like working here especially getting paid.

Mama's business was coming along great. Customers were coming already. She thanked everyone for their help and was so grateful for all that God has given her thus far. It's been about a week since we saw or heard from Victor. It feels good to see mama smile. She spends a lot of quality time with Joseph and Sophie more. She hasn't found her a new boo yet. Since I can remember mama always had a man by her side. This time I think that things has changed and it's not about men for her right now. It's just about the business and more about us kids. I'm overwhelmed with the attention that she is given us all. It has been way overdue and I'll take it.

I think I spoke Victor up too soon! We were just getting ready for dinner. When he came banging at the door demanding Sylvia to open it.

"Get away from my door, Victor!"

"Bitch, you're going to open this door and tell me what the hell did you do to me!" Mama told me to call Tio, then call the police.

"What the hell are you talking about Victor?"

"No, you mean what the hell you did to me? You knew that was my shop. You had no right to change the name!"

"Victor, you never once gave me any money towards this business. So how do you think that it's your shop? Did you even have any money to finance a business?"

"Shut up and open the door bitch! I want to look you in your face when I give you what I have for you."

"Leave it at the door. I'll get it later."

"No! Open this damn door now!" he started banging on it even harder. The super was up on the ladder hanging light bulbs. He told Victor that he can't be doing that in here. Mr. Hernandez told him that he has to leave the building. Victor turned around and shouted!

"I'm not going anywhere until I see the bitch in this apartment. At that moment, Mr. Hernandez started to come down from off the ladder. Before he could get all the way down, Victor saw Tio come from around the corner and the next thing you know, Victor started shooting. He shot Mr. Hernandez then turned to Uncle Frank and shot him in the upper torso. The cops heard the shooting as they were coming up the stairs. They saw

Victor holding the gun. Immediately, the cops told him to freeze and drop the gun, but he wouldn't. So, they shot him and he went down. Mama heard the shooting ran over to us screaming for us to go into the bathroom and lock the door! We all were so scared, because she did not know if Victor was going to get into the house. She heard the police. She looked out the peephole and saw Victor laying on the ground with the police surrounding him. Slowly, she opened the door and saw that he has shot her brother and Mr. Hernandez. She ran to her brother screaming, hollering, and crying hysterically, hoping, and praying that Victor didn't kill him.

"NO! NO! Frank!" she shouted. "No! (hermano) brother as she went down to the floor to see if he was alive. Sylvia cried,(hermano, hermano) brother brother. She cried please wake up. I can't lose you. Please Hermano wake up. Faintly, he opened his eyes. At that moment, he mumbled, "(hermana) sister I'm OK. That asshole got me in the shoulder."

He grazed Mr. Hernandez on the side of his stomach, but he broke his back falling off the ladder. Ambulances and fire trucks came and took my brother and Mr. Hernandez to the hospital. The coroner came for Victor, who was pronounce dead.

"I can't believe that that bastard came over here to kill me!" Mama said, "and in front of my kids! Was he going to kill us all? All for a business that he did not own, bought or care to put any money, blood, and sweat into?

I know that everything that glitters is not gold, and everything that looks pleasing to the eye is not good enough for you. Once they took Victor away it was a site of release for us all. Knowing that he won't come banging again.

A few days passed after that horrific incident and today was graduation. I was excited and glad because this day was finally here. The ceremony took forever. I did get some money for college. Terrance and Carla got scholarships. We all were so happy that we all made it through school with all our trials, family messes, and murders. We made it through!

Tio was doing well, and Mr. Hernandez was coming along too. After the incident with Victor, we moved into a nice, gated community with the help of mama lawyer friends. I still hold my breath, because I never know when mama will let another boo "thing" come into her life, and her old habits appear again.

I worked at mama's business and spent more time on my designs. Sylvia business gave her more time for herself. I found myself thinking about Carla and Terrance. I know that they will be leaving me soon and I won't be able to talk to them as often as I want. Talking to them both always seem to soothe my mind. We met up so that we could say goodbye to each other. We hugged, cried, and made a pack to always find time to meet up with each other on our college breaks. We, again, also promised that we will never stop being the CTT gang.

About the Author

Hello, my name is Serina Garland and I'm 57 years old. I was born and raised in Brooklyn, New York. At the age of nine, I lost my mother to breast cancer and was separated from my five siblings. As devastating as that was, it ironically caused me to grow up fast. So, after all of this, I needed to find a sense of belonging-which I will dive further into in my upcoming sophomore novel.

I found a passion for writing through my trials and tribulations throughout my 57 years of life. I put my love for writing on the back burner, I had to take time to find myself. As I was searching for true love, I ran into many Fakers, Breakers, and Takers that left me trying to figure myself out without knowing God is Love.
I went through many struggles to overcome my pain. We all fall down but it's how long you stay there that counts.

So, unless you know my story, "you will never understand my glory."
-Serina Garland

Serina Garland

Author contact information:

Email: serinabrown777@yahoo.com

@serina.brown.395

@mz_garland56

Made in the USA
Columbia, SC
31 August 2022

66351133R00148